KEEPING SCORE

A NOVEL BY

DEE LAGASSE

Cover Design by Kat Savage of Savage Hart Book Services
Edited by Christina Hart of Savage Hart Book Services
Proofread by Amanda Cuff of Savage Hart Book Services
Formatted by J.R. Rogue of Savage Hart Book Services

ISBN: 9798591051914
ASIN: B08HM9YG5K

For Travis Soucy, Amanda Masse, and Mark Rossetti.
There's something about childhood best friends that can never be replaced.
Thank you for being by my side then, now, and on all the days in between.

PROLOGUE

Isa

IF SOMEONE TOLD me at the beginning of my freshman year that being surrounded by shirtless football players wouldn't faze me, I would have called them a liar.

If they went on to tell me I'd be sitting comfortably on the shoulders of Jake Pierce—in a small black bikini, nonetheless—I would have laughed in their face. *Hysterically.*

Still, *somehow*, I ended up on Jake's shoulders during a game of *chicken.*

The concept was simple: lock hands with your opponent (positioned on *their* teammate's shoulders) and try to push them down into the water.

I shouldn't have lasted as long as I did. The guys we'd been going against were athletes. Most of them spent hours a day in the gym. I was fairly certain they could easily bench press me. But it seemed as if they were too scared to be rough with me.

"Eight and ohhhhh!" Jake called out triumphantly as Tommy Hannigan fell into the water. All six feet of Fox Hollow's star quarterback crashed down, creating enough of a splash that even I felt the impact. "Who wants next?"

"I didn't realize you were keeping score." I laughed, looking down just in time to see a devilish grin spread across my best friend's face. The same grin that made my heart beat faster and my stomach knot up.

"Always, Bug. Always."

Before anyone else had the chance to dethrone us as the "*chicken champions*," my father casually strolled over to the edge of the pool. The sight of him with a backward baseball hat and a black "The Grill Father" apron earned him a well-deserved eye roll.

"Food is ready!" His voice carried across the backyard so the twenty or so teenagers there could all hear him. "There's a pink platter. Do not eat that. That's the rabbit food for my favorite daughter."

This resulted in another even more dramatic eye roll before I called him out on the fact that I was his *only* daughter.

"Even more reason for you to be my favorite." He grinned as he waved me and Jake out of the pool. "C'mon, you two."

I hadn't noticed that Jake and I were the only ones left in the water.

Everyone else was already lined up at the food tables across the lawn. As Jake made his way out of the pool, with me still atop his shoulders, my legs tightened their wrap. In the pool, if I fell, I was going into the water. But I was *not* about to eat dirt in front of every senior on the Fox Hollow football team.

"Relax. I got you." Jake's hands clasped over my thighs as if to secure me.

The guilt of whatever I felt for Jake came creeping back in with his touch. It wasn't enough to mask the physical evidence of my body reacting to the warmth of his hands covering my cold, damp legs.

"Cold, Bug?" Jake teased. Reaching up, he placed his hands on each side of my waist. Effortlessly, he simultaneously crouched down and lifted me off his shoulders.

The soft green grass under my feet was comforting—and disappointing.

I didn't realize how close we were. When I turned, I found myself almost face-to-face with him. In a backyard full of football players, Jake was seemingly modest in height. Most of his teammates towered over him. With me at only five-foot-two though, all of them towered over me.

I fought the urge to fix the disheveled mop on his head. In the midst of all the graduation craziness, he allowed the black hair—both on his face and atop his head—to grow out. It was the first time in our friendship he wasn't sporting a clean faded haircut and a shaven face.

"I can hear you silently judging me, you know." Jake laughed as he dried his lower half off with a towel. "I have an appointment tomorrow to get it all cut off."

"Keep the facial hair." I shrugged once he looked up at me with raised eyebrows.

"Oh, you like the scruff?" he asked, running his hand against his jawline.

The knot in my stomach, a byproduct of the nerves I experienced only around Jake, made its return.

Distance.

I needed distance.

"Damnnnn. Will you two just fuck already?" Tommy laughed as he threw a punch into Jake's abs. All eight of them. "You can't use the excuse that she's Coach's daughter anymore, bro. Coach Coleman ain't your coach no more, 'Bama boooooy."

"I have a boyfriend," I shot back. The excuse was enough to end the conversation. For now.

Anyone with two seeing eyeballs could tell there was more than friendship between me and Jake. But if someone so much as *hinted* there could be more than a platonic friendship between me and Jake, I went into defense mode. It was mostly self-preservation at that point.

I had accepted that I felt something for Jake sometime during our sophomore year. It was a mix of physical and emotional attraction I assumed would dwindle if not acted upon. *(Spoiler alert: it didn't.)* I figured Jake just didn't feel the same way about me.

I wasn't exactly his type. The girls Jake dated wore Abercrombie, had fake tans, and always had their nails done. My wardrobe consisted mostly of ripped jeans and band tees. My nails were always cut short and painted black—which I did myself, *thank you very much*.

My makeup was almost never done. It seemed silly to put on layers of concealer and foundation only to sweat it off at the skate park.

I just wasn't the kind of girl Jake Pierce liked.

I accepted that and I moved on. Mostly.

"Shut the fuck up, Tommy," Jake added.

The warning in his tone wasn't something I heard too often. His eyes narrowed as Tommy stepped back. With a slight shake of his head, Tommy sprinted to the line of teenage boys waiting for food.

The four long banquet tables I helped my brother set up earlier that day were now filled with trays of food, bowls of salads, chip bags, and sodas. Behind said tables were my parents, my brother, my abuela, and the Fox Hollow coaching staff—all scattered about, assisting as needed.

For as long as I can remember, my parents have thrown a "Senior Bye-B.Q." every July for members of the football team. It

didn't matter if they were a player that started every single game—
like Jake had—or if they were the team photographer like me; if
you had a role on the team, you were invited.

Normally, I'd be on the other side of the table with my family
too. My dad wouldn't hear of it this year. I was allowed to help set
up, but the moment the players from the team started to show up,
he instructed me to "*go have fun.*"

Football had been over since November. So, despite the fact
that we all went to the same school, we hadn't been together in
one place since the post-season awards banquet. Plus, the
atmosphere in my parents' backyard was much more relaxed than
the hotel ballroom had been.

The banquet turned into something of a press conference
when Jake and Tommy accepted awards and announced where they
would be attending college. I already knew Jake had accepted a full
scholarship to the University of Alabama. In fact, I was the one
that straightened his crimson-colored tie before he walked up to
the podium.

Admittedly, it was much easier to focus that day, considering
his muscles were hidden behind his shirt.

"Nice tattoo." As I put space between us, I tried desperately to
change the subject.

There always seemed to be an awkward lull of silence between
us after anyone questioned our bond. However, I knew if we didn't
move on by the time we made our way to the food tables, someone
in my family would call us out on acting weird.

The week-old ink on Jake's back wasn't his only tattoo. The day
he turned eighteen in April, he got a fox on his forearm.

On my eighteenth birthday last week, he took me to get the
Jack Skellington now permanently inked into my left shoulder
blade. What I didn't expect was for him to pop into the chair right

after me and get a tattoo of Sally in the same spot. We'd joked before about getting matching best friend tattoos a few times, but I never thought he was serious.

"I could say the same to you." He chuckled. "Has Abuela forgiven you yet?"

"As soon as she found out you got Sally, it was fine," I said as we inched our way toward the first table of food. "Speaking of your biggest fan..."

At the sight of Jake approaching the table, Abuela's entire face lit up. After dropping the tongs she'd been using to serve her famous enchiladas, she began to make her way around the table. For a woman in her seventies, she sure could move quickly to get to us.

I call it: *The Jake Pierce Effect.*

"Hola, Jacob!" my abuela exclaimed with open arms.

Without hesitation, Jake wrapped my grandmother in his arms. Beating her to the punch, he kissed her on the cheek before he let her go.

"Oh hi, Abuela." I waved both of my hands, signaling my presence. "I'm here too. You know, your only granddaughter."

"Si, of course, mi mariquita." A grin spread across her face. Her nose scrunched as she planted a kiss on my cheek, undoubtedly leaving the mark of her trademark red lipstick. "Pero, Jacob is leaving us dentro un poco."

"You won't be able to get rid of me that easily," Jake assured her as he reached for a plate and plastic utensils. He handed them to me before taking his own and then moved down the table. "Where else am I going to get tamales?"

"I'm sure there will be Mexican restaurants in Alabama, *Jacob*," I teased, scooping my dad's homemade macaroni salad onto my plate.

I didn't start calling Jake his full first name until after I heard my grandmother say it while doting on him. She was the only person that called him Jacob. Typically, as soon as she'd turn her back, Jake would flip me off. Since her eyes were still fixed on the two of us, he stuck his tongue out before turning back and then winked at Abuela.

"But they won't be as good as Abuela's," he said. He skipped right over all the traditional American barbecue food and went right to the trays of food my mom and abuela spent the last two days preparing. As he scooped a heaving pile of rice onto his plate, he offered my mom an ear-to-ear grin. "Or Mama Alma's rice."

"There's nothing as good as the real thing," my dad agreed as he wrapped his arms around my mom's waist.

I didn't bother to argue that.

I learned at a young age that America's version of Mexican food and *authentic* Mexican food could be vastly different...and the real thing was almost always better.

Once our plates were full—or in Jake's case, *plates*—we joined a group of guys sitting on the deck that overlooked the backyard. Without being asked, three of them stood up at once and offered me their spot at the table. I waved them all off, taking a seat on the warm wooden planks below.

After we ate, we hopped into an ongoing game of lawn volleyball. How Jake could eat multiple plates of heavy food and jump around immediately afterward was baffling. Volleyball somehow turned into a big free-for-all football game. Jake and Tommy were made captains, and after three very intense rounds of *rock, paper, scissors*, Tommy got to select his first player.

It was of no surprise to anyone that he chose me.

"Such bullshit," Jake muttered under his breath as I stood behind Tommy.

The thought of him being upset that I wasn't on his team made me happier than it should have. Tommy picked up on Jake's annoyance and utilized it to our team's advantage. It was no accident I was put in Jake's path during more than one play. The longer the game went on, the more Jake seemed to relax.

By the time he had the opportunity to stop me from scoring—by picking me up and running with me slung over his shoulder across the yard—he was as cool as a cucumber.

"Personal foul!" I yelled, while everyone looked on and laughed. "Where's the ref?!"

He looked real smug as he placed me back on the ground in his team's end zone.

Until the sound of a whistle blowing caught our attention. My parents both walked across the lawn until they joined the group of onlookers. My dad looked at my mom and nodded.

At that, she called, "Personal foul. Defense. Fifteen-yard penalty. Automatic first down."

"Booyah!" I raised my hands in triumph as I did something that was supposed to resemble a victory dance.

"All right, all right." Jake pushed me playfully. "You wanna play? Come on, Bug. Let's play."

Something in Jake shifted as we played. His touch was less gentle. Not enough to hurt me, but he certainly wasn't apologetic when his hand grazed across my ass as he ran past me. The way he hungrily looked down at my body when we stood across each other had my head spinning. So much so that I started to move before the snap of the ball.

"False start!" my dad called from the mock sideline. "Offense. Five-yard penalty."

"What's the matter, Isa?" Jake teased lowly. "Can't focus?"

"Someone can play for me!" I called out. "I need water."

As I walked away from the formation to the cooler full of bottled water, I could feel the intensity of Jake's stare on my back. I didn't rejoin the game.

For the next couple of hours, we kept our distance from each other. But as the afternoon rolled into evening, the crowd dwindled down until Jake was the last player left. It wasn't surprising he was the only one to stick around. However, it made keeping him at arm's length a little harder.

"Shouldn't you be heading to Kelsie's?" I asked, scooping rice into the Tupperware container my mother had handed me moments before.

At this point, most of the team had moved on to Kelsie Madden's house for a keg party. As much as I tried to hide my disgust when the name of Jake's on-again, off-again girlfriend left my lips, there was no way to hide the downward curl of my snarl.

I didn't hate many people and, in the grand scheme of things, Kelsie and Jake made sense. For our last two years of high school, Kelsie was the captain of the cheer squad. Jake was a record-breaking, starting wide receiver for the Fox Hollow Cubs. Where Jake was kindhearted and genuine, Kelsie was conniving and as fake as the platinum blonde hair on her head.

I experienced that firsthand a few weeks ago when she started a rumor that I slept with every member of Sulking Skulls—the rock band my boyfriend Devon played bass guitar for. Everyone knew it was bullshit. Kelsie even admitted to Jake that the only reason she even started it was because she was mad he went to prom with me instead of her.

Mind you, they never had plans to go together, and they were on one of their "breaks" anyway. Jake ended things for good with her shortly after when she tried to slither her way back in. Jake had enough respect for her to do it quietly. Kelsie wouldn't have that, though.

She showed up to our high school graduation the following day, hysterical, telling anyone who'd listen that Jake broke up with her *"so he could have as much college pussy as he wanted."*

"I'm supposed to make an appearance." He sounded less than thrilled about the idea. Until his eyes lit up. "Wanna come?"

The hope in his voice was almost enough to get me to say yes. *Almost.*

"To watch you get drunk and make-out with half the cheer squad?" I scoffed quietly, since my parents were within earshot.

When the last of the rice was packed up, I grabbed a slice of watermelon and a can of soda. Jake followed me into the separately fenced-in portion of our yard that contained the pool.

Taking a seat at the edge of the pool, I let my feet dangle above the water. "No thanks."

"So, where's Douchey Devon tonight?" he countered.

He didn't bother to hide the disdain in his voice.

He didn't *ever* hide his belief that I could do better than Devon.

Where Jake and I didn't make sense on paper, Devon and I did. We ran in the same circles. We had similar taste in clothing, music, and art. I just didn't know how long it would last with the two of us. In the mere few weeks' time of our relationship, I had questioned whether or not to end things more than once.

The sneaky, unjustifiable emotions that flooded me whenever Jake was around certainly didn't help matters either.

"I don't know." I shrugged. "He was supposed to call me after band practice but—"

I stopped myself, knowing if I were to continue it'd only result in a lecture. Not soon enough, though.

"You deserve so much better." The goosebumps returned when he placed his hand on my thigh. The quick motion of his hand moving back and forth was meant to be reassuring. My body didn't get the memo, though. His hand was cold and wet from the frosty can of Pepsi he'd been holding. The contrast of it against my warm sun-kissed skin sent my senses into instant overdrive. "Cold?"

"Yes," I lied. I hadn't been in the pool in hours. And although the sun had already set, the humid summer air still hung heavy around us.

"Liar," he whispered.

I could feel his eyes focused on my face as he waited for my response.

"Excuse me?" I shot back defensively. My brows furrowed as I turned to face him. "I'm a lot of things, but a liar is not—"

Before I could finish my sentence, Jake's hands cupped my face. His lips crashed down onto mine, the sneak attack of a kiss rendering me completely frozen.

The initial shock wore off as fast as it set in. The watermelon that lingered on his lips and the tenderness of his touch pulled me under like a tidal wave. Feverishly and without abandon, his tongue danced over mine. With every passing moment, I felt myself slipping further and further into the depths of our kiss.

Nothing else mattered. No one else mattered.

"While I hate to be the one that breaks this up, I thought you might want to know Devon is at the front door. Mom's keeping him busy, but..."

The sound of my older brother's voice behind us was like a wrecking ball breaking our contact.

In the process of jumping up, I accidentally kicked one of cans of soda into the pool. "Fuck!" I cursed. The sinking realization of what just happened settled in my stomach when I said, "Oh my God. *Devon.*"

I just cheated on Devon. I kissed Jake.

Well, *technically*, Jake kissed me, but I fucking kissed him back. I kissed him back and I didn't think twice. I didn't stop it. I didn't *want* to stop it.

"Break up with him," Jake said, as if it were the most obvious thing in the world. He grabbed my hand and gave it a small squeeze. "I fucking love you, Isa. You have to know that by now. Be with me. We can figure everything else out later."

I knew it couldn't be that simple.

I knew it, and I said okay anyway.

"You know I can't be around Devon, especially after that. I should probably head out. The guys are expecting me. I have to at least make an appearance." He shrugged, rolling his eyes. After letting go of my hand, he grinned, excitement rolling off him as the dread of facing Devon filled me. "Let's meet at our spot in the morning."

I nodded, and then watched him jog across the lawn and carefully open the latch of the chain-link fence. The sudden need to say the words waiting on the tip of my tongue hit me as he was about to step out of the yard.

"Jake!" When he didn't turn, I called him by the one thing I knew would get his attention. *"Jacob!"*

At the sound of his full name, he stopped. As he turned to face me, I swallowed. This was the moment. This was the moment that would change everything.

"Yessss?" he asked. His voice trailed in the distance between us.

"I love you too."

ISA

Six Years Later...

"Whatever plans you have tonight...cancel them. I need you on the VIP floor. The Bluecoats will be in the house tonight."

Looking up from my well-loved copy of *Interview with a Vampire*, I raised my brow in annoyance.

As soon as I saw my brother standing in the doorframe, a dramatic huff of a sigh expelled from my lips. The pleading look in his eyes told me everything he wasn't saying—that this was last-minute and he'd have to scramble to find someone else if I didn't say yes.

After marking my page with a bookmark, I closed my book. "You're the Director of Entertainment at the biggest nightclub in Boston. You'd think you would have found some photographer friends by now." I stood to shoo him out of the room. "One of these nights, I'm actually going to have plans and you're going to be shit out of luck, Javi."

"Have I told you lately that you're my favorite sister?" he said, beaming as he turned to leave. The sound of his voice boomed when he called out, "We leave in an hour and a half! Iced chai's on me."

"I'm your *only* sister!" I yelled back before pushing my bedroom door shut.

I grabbed a pair of cutoff black jean shorts from my dresser and then stripped out of the poplin pajama pants I'd changed into just an hour ago. After spending most of my afternoon taking photographs of the most misbehaved children I'd met in my entire life, I *was* excited to spend the rest of the night in bed.

I could have said no to Javier. He knew I wouldn't, though. Now that I had a gallery lease to pay for, I was taking every job I could until the grand opening next month. Even if it meant dealing with horribly behaved kids and demanding mothers who barked out orders behind me.

Not that I minded working at Retro for my brother. The pay was great; the exposure was even better. I was there enough that people started to recognize me, and the photography credits on Retro's social media posts sent new followers my way every weekend.

Once I found one of my staff T-shirts, I swapped out my camisole for a black padded push-up bra. Krissy, one of the bartenders, had taken all my work shirts and cut the necklines out. They now hung off my shoulders, and scooped down low enough to show what little cleavage I had. For the bartenders and shot girls, it was a way to make a little more money. For me, it was a way to uniform us as one and stand together as the women of Retro. I didn't really see how cutting up fabric brought us all together, but I was happy to be considered part of the Retro crew.

After pulling my hair up into a high ponytail, I quickly did my makeup. I spent so much time outside over the last couple of months, the sun-kissed glow on my skin eliminated any need for concealer or foundation. But after dramatically winging my liquid eyeliner, I cursed under my breath when one looked drastically better than the other.

This. Always. Happened.

There wasn't time to fix it a hundred more times, though. So, begrudgingly, I left it as it was.

It was only after adding a few layers of thick black mascara to my lashes and a final pop of bright red to my lips that I decided I was good to go.

My area of the house was considered its own apartment, even if the two doors that separated the two floors of the house were never closed. When my brother and his fiancé mentioned they were thinking about renting out the lower level of their house, conveniently, the lease on my apartment was just about to end.

Instead of signing another lease for the tiny studio apartment I had in Boston, I packed up all my things and moved into the basement of my brother's new house. For the most part, we co-existed as two separate households. With the exception of a kitchen, I had everything I could need downstairs. We even converted the unfinished storage area into a dark room for my photography.

Though, *comfortable* wouldn't exactly be the word I'd use to describe how I felt walking into the kitchen. The conversation Javier and Adam were having about what to get my grandmother for her upcoming birthday came to an immediate halt when Adam's eyes widened. As my brother turned to see what caught Adam's attention, I let out a small laugh.

"Dang, mamacita!" Adam praised. His nod of approval gave me the reassurance I didn't even know I needed. "Look at you work the Retro tee!"

As expected, a scowl spread across my brother's lips immediately. "Absolutely not. No sister of mine—"

"Will what?" I crossed my arms in disapproval, stopping my

brother before he finished his sentence and challenging him as I continued. "Look like every other woman employed at Retro? Yes. Yes, she will."

"She's got you there, babe." Adam chuckled, and I *knew* he'd be on my side. He usually was. Over time, he became like another brother to me, but he tended to be a little more subjective about things than Javier. "You can't give her a hard time when all the rest of the girls are wearing tiny booty shorts and cut up shirts. At least Isa's shorts don't show her coochie."

"All right!" Javier raised his hands in defeat. "But can we never, and I mean *never*, say the words 'Isa' and 'coochie' in the same sentence again?"

I shook my head then asked, "Are you ready?"

Despite the two of us working at the same place tonight, Javier's outfit looked nothing like mine.

The slim white dress slacks and loafers were quite the contrast from the five-dollar thrift store shorts and old high-top Converse All-Stars I had on. However, the fitted green button-up shirt he wore matched the neon Retro logo on the corner of my shirt. So, there was that.

"Are you ready?" he mimicked. "I've been waiting on you, hermana."

I waved goodbye to Adam, then followed my brother out of the side door off the kitchen.

As I stepped onto the red wooden deck, I was blasted with the late afternoon sunshine. The dry air and thick humidity settled in my lungs in the few short seconds it took me to get settled in the passenger seat of Javier's Lexus.

"Are you excited?" he asked, turning to face me as he turned the key in the ignition.

A growing smirk spread across his lips, reminding me of the Cheshire Cat from *Alice in Wonderland*.

"About work?" I brushed the comment off, feigning innocence. "It's a job, Javi. I know how to be professional."

I knew why he was asking.

I also knew that even if he had enough photographers, he would have found a way to get me inside the club tonight.

Because if there was anything I loved as much as photography, it was football.

Football has always been a part of my life. I was only three when my dad retired from the NFL, but he didn't even take a season off before he started coaching Fox Hollow's high school team. All of our weekends were taken up by football growing up.

Friday nights were spent at the high school games he coached. Saturday, we watched college football. Before I even knew Alabama was a state, I knew that in our house, we rooted for the Crimson Tide.

Sundays were my favorite, though. Our house was always full on Sundays. Javier and I would wear matching jerseys. It wasn't until I was about eight when I realized *why* it was so damn cool to have my last name on the back. That was roughly the time my parents realized I was no longer coloring in my Disney Princess books on the living room floor.

The laughter that erupted from my father when I stood up and yelled at the receiver to *"run the freakin' ball"* is something I'd never forget for the rest of my life. Before the game was over, my dad made a few calls and got us tickets right on the fifty-yard line and field passes for an upcoming game.

That was it for me.

I was in love.

And, Javier knew how much I loved it.

He knew—for me—being a Coleman meant taking pride in the legacy our father created. He didn't love the game the way my dad and I did, but he understood it was more than just about the sport. Football was more than four quarters and touchdowns for me.

It was the rush of dopamine when your favorite team scored. It was the moment you held your breath and prayed there was enough time left on the clock for one more play. It was triumph and pride after wins. Disappointment after losses.

Football was a *feeling*.

Thanks to my dad, I'd been lucky enough to meet some of the greatest players in the game. I'd been to Super Bowls and gotten to walk the carpet at the ESPYs—the Grammys of the sports world. As I got older, the players in the game started phasing out, and newer, younger players took their place.

There were even a few times I'd caught the attention of a player at an event. The moment they learned I was Roger Coleman's daughter, they found an excuse to back out of the conversation. It was like that growing up as *"Coach's daughter"* too.

Which was why I turned in my seat and faced my brother. "Can we maybe not mention who our dad is, though? I love Dad, but I just feel like everyone looks at me differently as soon as they realize I'm Roger Coleman's daughter."

"Well...I think I should probably tell you..." he started. After offering me a small smile, he quickly stammered out, "It was Jake that called me."

Well, fuck.

A surge of panic jolted through me.

I knew this day would come eventually. It was inevitable. Unavoidable.

Jake Pierce was my best friend.

Keyword: was.

Jake Pierce and I first met when we were in the same kindergarten class. Our paths crossed again in second grade, third grade, and fifth grade. We even had some classes together in middle school, but our friendship didn't truly begin until our freshman year of high school.

Jake was the first freshman in the history of Fox Hollow High School to not only make the varsity team but also start in his very first game. I was the team's photographer. He asked about my camera one day, and our friendship blossomed from there. It didn't take us long to become inseparable.

Jake Pierce was my best friend...*until the day I broke his fucking heart.*

ISA

I PULLED my cell phone out of the camera bag that sat on the floorboard at my feet.

After opening my text messages, I tapped the very first one at the top of the screen.

Me: Guess who's going to be at Retro tonight?

Three little dots appeared on the bottom of the screen immediately. They stopped and started again three times before my phone vibrated in my hands. Right on cue, my best friend's face showed up on the screen.

I declined the call to quickly text instead.

Me: In the car with Javi. Can't talk.

Salem: Okay. So...we knew this day would come when he was traded. Where's your head at?

Salem was also in Mrs. Tillman's kindergarten class with me and Jake. We both showed up on the first day of school with the same Scooby-Doo backpack and decided right then and there that we were best friends. That simple decision gifted us almost twenty years of friendship.

Her house became my second home, and she was given a spare

key to my parents' house. While we were growing up, we fought like sisters. But, man, we loved like sisters too. Which was why when Jake kissed me and I broke up with Devon, Salem was the one I called.

We were in the middle of a fight. Looking back, I don't even remember what it was about. I just remember calling her sobbing and her showing up fifteen minutes later. We hadn't gotten in a single fight since then.

Me: All over the place.

Me: Like, what do I even say to him?

Salem: I don't know. You might want to start with sorry, though.

Damn her and her blunt honesty.

"Where's your head at, hermana?"

My brother's choice of words as he pulled into the drive-thru of Pressed Café made me laugh.

"Salem just asked the same thing," I explained, due to the lift of his brow at my response. "I don't know. It's been a long time. I don't even know what I'm supposed to say to him."

After rattling off our drink order into the speaker box, Javier pulled forward slightly. There were two cars ahead of us. Just enough time for a mini brotherly pep talk.

"You know, I try really hard not to be the kind of brother that tells you what you should do..." His voice trailed and then he paused.

"But?" I added, knowing it was coming next.

"You owe him an apology." My brother sighs as one of the cars ahead of us pulled away from the pick-up window. The brief silence that filled the car while we inched forward in line was just enough to brace myself for what I knew he was about to say. "Or at the very least, an explanation. I heard him—that night by the pool. I heard him tell you he loved you. And, I heard you say you loved him too."

"Javier—" I opened my mouth to defend myself, promptly closing it again when I realized I didn't actually *have* a defense.

Over the course of the next few minutes, my brother smiled politely and made small talk with the barista working inside the coffee shop. I sat silently as he took our drinks from the window and paid. My mind raced once he pulled out of the drive-thru and picked up right where he left off.

"You told him you would meet him in the morning, and you didn't. I mean, I get it. It was probably a lot to deal with. Especially all at once. But the boy told you he *loved* you, Isa, and you responded by avoiding his phone calls and sneaking out the back door when you heard him in the house. I don't know if I'll ever forget the hope and then the sadness on his face when he realized you weren't in the car with us to say goodbye before he left for Alabama."

"I was eighteen!" I shouted, like that completely justified my actions. "Do you think it was easy for me? He was my best friend too, Javi. I didn't know what I was feeling. When I figured it out, it was too late."

"You still love him."

There was no question in my brother's statement. Maybe he'd known for a long time.

At least since the night I decided getting wasted on cheap vodka was better than acknowledging that Jake had posted a picture of him kissing another girl. We were about a month into our freshman year of college. Jake was in Alabama. Salem and I were at the University of Massachusetts together.

Despite her pleas to stay in our dorm room, I decided I needed to go find a party. Before I could do anything too stupid, Salem called my brother. Javier showed up at the frat house I had wandered into. I fought him kicking and screaming until he threatened to call my parents. That was also the first night I met Adam.

To this day, I'd always been so thankful he didn't judge me based on first impressions.

I spent the entire twenty-minute car ride to his apartment drunkenly spewing the ugliest things about a girl I'd never met.

I hated her.

I hated everything about her.

I hated her bright pink Polo shirt—with every button undone, and the collar popped up. She had on the tiniest white shorts. Her bleach blonde hair was pulled into a high ponytail on the top of her head, much like my own right now.

I hated that Jake clearly had a type.

Pretty. Blonde-haired. Blue-eyed. Cheerleader.

I hated that she was everything I wasn't.

But more than that...I hated that she was everything I wanted to be.

Not that I wanted to be a blonde-haired, blue-eyed cheerleader. I was always quite content with my ripped jeans, band tees, and Chucks. There was never a time I didn't love my hips and the "*bubble butt*" my mom said I inherited from her.

But that girl had Jake. His attention. His time. *His lips on hers.*

And after that night, she just kept showing up in his photos.

Salem and I dubbed her "Alabama Barbie" before we found out her name was Jess and that she was *actually* from Ohio.

Based on the evidence that they seemed to be at a party every single time Jake posted photos of the two of them together, I didn't think they were that serious. I thought I had a chance to fix things. I had a plan.

I waited for him to show up at my parents' house on Christmas Eve. After all, it was tradition. But he never came.

Instead, Jake brought Jess back to Massachusetts to meet his mom. My parents ran into the three of them at the grocery store the day after Christmas and invited them over for dinner. Despite the fact that I was staying in my old bedroom during break, I found an excuse to leave.

I didn't want to see Jake. More importantly, I didn't want to see Jake with *her*.

I became quite the expert in excuse-making since then. Because of that, I successfully managed to avoid Jake for the last six years. It helped that he lived in Alabama, then in Florida, and—according to my father—spent the majority of the most recent off-season in Montana.

There was no reasonable way to explain why it still terrified me —the thought of seeing him.

Maybe it was because I knew I'd have to explain myself.

Maybe it was because Salem and Javier were right: Jake deserved an apology.

Maybe, just maybe, I was simply scared to face him because I knew it didn't matter how much time had passed.

It hadn't changed what he meant to me.

It was easier to push it aside, to pretend those feelings didn't exist, when I didn't have to face him.

I missed him.

It was as simple and as complicated as that.

I missed what we had together. There were no walls between us. No secrets. No boundaries. Everything Jake and I shared, was genuine.

There were still times I found myself wishing I could just pick up the phone and call him. We were each other's biggest fans. We got each other through the hard days. When Jake said everything was going to be okay, I believed him.

It wasn't that I didn't try to move on. I tried to forget him. There was nothing I wanted more than to just put the past behind me, but it was hard to let go of someone when they invaded your dreams. *Every fucking night.*

It also didn't help that he maintained a relationship with every person in my family. My parents, my brother, and my abuela never thought twice to turn on the television when they knew he was playing a game. My father was with Jake when he was drafted. Everyone, except me, flew to Miami for his first game as a professional football player. My parents were Jake's personal guests for the Super Bowl.

For more than half a decade, I watched Jake play from behind a television screen. I saw him grow as a player—both on and off the field. I heard the post-game interviews when he took both the wins and the losses with the same grace.

I'd seen the photos of him visiting children's hospitals. On Father's Day, my dad was late to his own barbecue because he attended a charity golf game Jake hosted to raise funds for Fox Hollow's youth football programs.

Part of me wished he turned into an egomaniac when he was drafted. There was also a small sliver of unexplainable hope that my family would cut ties altogether. It was completely selfish of me. Jake didn't deserve that.

It probably would have stopped the *what ifs,* though.

What if I had answered his calls the night he kissed me? What if I met him at our spot the next day? What if I had listened to my heart instead of my head? Would we have stayed together? Would we still be together to this day? What if he still held it against me?

What if he doesn't forgive me?

ISA

IT WAS EARLY ENOUGH that once we got into the city, there was no need to rush. Neither Javier nor I said a word as we walked the three blocks from the parking garage to the club. Which was fine by me. The thoughts in my head were loud enough to drown out the buzz of Boston's rush hour traffic.

When we reached Retro, I was surprised to see a line forming outside already. The doors wouldn't even open to clubgoers for another two hours. It wasn't out of the ordinary to come into work on Friday and Saturday nights and find people waiting to get in, but it was five o'clock. *On a Tuesday.* It was still light out.

As we approached a group of scantily dressed women, I couldn't help but notice that half of them were wearing body-hugging Bluecoats football jerseys.

"Hi, I'm Isa Coleman, one of the Retro house photographers. Do you ladies mind if I grab a picture to throw up on Instagram?"

They eagerly agreed. As they shifted and popped their hips, I counted down from three.

"Is it true?" one of them asked as soon as I snapped the photo. "Are the Mendez brothers and Jake Pierce inside?"

Stepping in, Javier redirected her question by offering their first round of drinks on the house. "Just tell the bartender it's on Javier."

The atmosphere in the club was nothing like it would be later that night.

Right then, bright fluorescent lights were lighting up the empty dance floor. In a few hours, they'd be turned off and replaced with the strobing neon kind. Luke Bryan's southern twang would be nonexistent and the bumping bass that came with nineties hip-hop would fill the speakers instead.

Bartenders and shot girls were either running back and forth restocking alcohol or setting up their stations for the night. A handful of bouncers who'd shown up already were all congregating in one corner, management in another.

Ace, the weeknight DJ, stood by the bar with an armful of bottled waters. As I approached, his eyes lit up in recognition. "Hey, Isa! I didn't know you were working." The corners of his lips curled up in a sly smile. "I actually have something for you tonight." Excited, he thanked Krissy, the bartender, for his water and made his way toward the DJ booth, which was set high on a platform overlooking the room.

Ace started as the weeknight DJ just a few weeks after I officially became one of the house photographers. I didn't work many weeknights, but I worked enough that I knew he played a "House Mix" for the staff while everyone got ready for their shift. From upper management to the bathroom attendants, if you were working, he wanted to make sure you were included.

Every time we worked together, he tried to get me to talk about the music I listened to. I brushed him off when I realized there was no one else in the building that shared my personal preference.

"All right," Ace began, his voice booming through the speakers as he spoke. There were maybe two dozen of us in the club that could hold just over a thousand people. "So, you guys know I've been working on figuring Isa out. Well, I got a tip from a little birdie, and I expect you all in the middle of the floor for the next couple of songs."

As "What's My Age Again" by blink-182 began to play, I looked around, ready to put the blame on my brother only to come up empty. Javier was nowhere to be found.

"Put that camera to the side, girlfriend." Krissy laughed as she gently hip-checked me. "You heard the man. He expects us to dance."

I slid one of my arms through the strap hanging loosely from my neck, double-checking to make sure my camera was secure. When I was certain it was okay, I grinned and took Krissy's outstretched hand.

By the time the first chorus hit, we were joined by three more bartenders and just as many bouncers. As the song came to an end, Ace seamlessly mixed in the live version of "Dammit"—also by blink-182, my favorite band since I was thirteen.

Back then, I thought I was such a badass while cursing with Mark Hoppus and Tom DeLonge as they sang. Travis Barker was the first celebrity I really crushed on. I'd seen them live more times than any other band. Even after Tom left the band in 2015, I went to every show faithfully.

When I was feeling especially nostalgic, I pulled out my old *The Mark, Tom, and Travis Show* CD and blasted it as loud as my car stereo allowed. Listening to it in my car was nothing like this, though—the music so clear it almost felt like I was at a concert.

Just like I would at a live show, I submerged myself into drum beats and guitar riffs. When the second verse started, I spun, my hands raised high above my head as I danced to the beat. Nostalgia coursed through my veins.

All of that stopped the moment I came face-to-face with the person I'd been hiding from for just over half a decade.

Jacob James Pierce.

I should have known as soon as I heard "Dammit" that the "*little birdie*" Ace mentioned was Jake. He was probably the only person on this earth that knew it was my favorite song. Everyone else in my life knew that blink-182 was my favorite band, but Jake was the one that spent hours with me listening to Dude Ranch on vinyl.

Jake was the one that knew everything.

Every damn thing that mattered.

When I pictured this moment in my head, I always imagined I would hold my head high and take responsibility for what I did. I didn't foresee the tight knots in my stomach or the small beads of sweat growing in my palms. The anticipation was laced with paralyzing fear. As soon as Javier told me—as soon as I began to panic —I should have known I wouldn't be able to handle this the way I presumed I could.

I should have known that Jake would make every nerve of my body go into overdrive. It was Jake, after all. How fucking foolish I had been to think he wouldn't still affect me like this.

With crossed arms and a knowing smirk, Jake nodded his head in the direction of the bar. I didn't say a word as I followed his lead. With every step we took, my heart slammed against my chest.

Thump, thump, thump.

And...why the fuck was it so damn hot in here?

When Jake stopped at the end of the bar, I prayed to all things holy that my shaky legs didn't give out beneath me.

Somehow, none of the photos or video coverage over the years had done Jake justice. The sleeves of his white V-neck hugged the bulging muscles of his biceps. I realized this when I caught myself staring at them like some sort of horny fangirl.

The next thing that grabbed my attention were the black skinny jeans he was wearing. I immediately had to fight the urge to call him out on his attire.

The boy I once knew had teased me about the ninety percent of guys I found attractive, using the argument that *"no guy's jeans should be tighter than his girlfriend's."*

But, he was not the boy I once knew.

He was also not dressed for a night at Retro.

Professional football player or not, there was a strictly enforced "no white shoes" rule in place at the club. His bright white Nikes made him a walking, talking contradiction. It was also too early—way too early—for him to be here.

"Jake!" I forced a big, *fake* smile in his direction. "Hi. It's so good to see you!"

At my response, his lips formed into a tight line. His brow furrowed in frustration as he let out a breath. "Don't do that." Breaking his eye contact with me, he asked the closest bartender if it was possible to get two shots of tequila.

For a brief moment, I assumed one of them was intended for me. I opened my mouth to tell him I couldn't drink while working, but he quickly downed both shots.

After pulling out his wallet, he dropped a few bills down by the empty shot glasses. "Don't act like you're excited to see me. We both know that's bullshit."

I swallowed, and the guilt that'd been building up over the last six years settled in my stomach like a brick. A top-forty country song started to play for one of the shot girls as I tried to find words. *Any words.*

None came.

Not a single word.

It was as if I'd forgotten the last twenty-four years of putting my thoughts into verbally spoken sentences.

"Don't worry. I won't be here long," he continued, unfazed by my silence. "I just brought Fox and Lynx by to check out the space for their thirtieth birthday."

Often said to be this generation's Peyton and Eli, Fox and Lynx Mendez quickly became Bluecoats favorites after they were the first twin brothers drafted to the same team in NFL history. Everyone in Fox Hollow thought it was meant to be, a gift from the football gods that Fox came to join our team. Given what he'd done for the Bluecoats, I wouldn't argue with them. It made sense that Jake would be friends with both of them.

The Mendez brothers were older than us, but that didn't matter on the field. As part of the offensive line, they all worked together—Fox as the starting quarterback, Lynx a wide receiver like Jake. I met Fox a few times when I attended games with my dad, but Lynx was much more elusive.

During my silent meltdown, I wondered how much of an asshole I'd be if I asked Jake to make introductions.

The thought was immediately abandoned when Jake offered me a small, sad smile. "Have a nice night. You look good, Bug."

A flood of emotions filled me when he called me by the nickname he gave me as a teenager. The memory of the moment crashed down on me like a tidal wave.

"You're just a little Shutterbug, aren't you?" he said as I snapped another photo. "From now on, I'm just gonna call you Bug."

"Bug?" I laughed nervously. "Really? Like an ant?"

"I was thinking more like a cute little ladybug that always has a camera hanging from her neck."

"My abuela calls me 'Mariquita,'" I started as I turned to face him. *"It means ladybug."*

"Well, now I have no choice." He shrugged. The corners of his lips turned up into a smile. *"It was meant to be, Bug."*

"Jake, wait!" I called out as he walked away from the bar. When he didn't turn, my nerves morphed into desperation. *"Jacob!"*

That got his attention. As he turned, I swallowed again, the pain visible on his face.

He shook his head slowly, lips forming a thin line. After a brief moment of thought, he closed the space he'd just put between us. "You don't get to do that, Isa. You don't get to call out my name like it pains you to say it."

"I'm sorry." I needed him to know. I needed him to know just how sorry I was. "I should have—"

"It was a long time ago." His tone was cold. Emotionless. A complete contradiction from the hurt his voice held just moments prior. "We were kids, Isa. I loved you. You chose Devon."

"I didn't *choose* Devon!" I yelled. The outburst drew attention to us. The feeling of people watching burned like fire on my skin. I didn't care, though. He was wrong. "I broke up with Devon the night you kissed me. I just needed time to wrap my head around what I felt for you. It scared me. *You* scared me."

"Wait, what? No," he said, shaking his head again, this time in disbelief. "Devon came to Kelsie's party a few hours later, bragging to the guys on the team about smashing Coach's daughter. I assumed that you...and when you didn't show up the next day, and you started avoiding me, I just..."

His sentences were fragments of unfinished thoughts, but I easily filled in the blanks as he went along. "You mean to tell me this whole time you thought I blew you off because I was too busy screwing Devon McDaniels?" I couldn't help but laugh, stopping only once I locked eyes with Jake, who apparently failed to see the humor in that I was still very much a virgin then.

"I need to find Javier." Jake didn't explain himself further before he left me there, standing alone.

As he walked away, the sounds of the club became increasingly louder. I'd been so hyper-focused on Jake, I almost forgot there were other people in the room with us.

"You must be the infamous Isabel."

While I was chasing my rampant thoughts, Lynx Mendez joined me by the bar.

"I am," I confirmed as I turned, sticking my hand out for him to take. "It's nice to meet you, Lynx."

Fox and Lynx Mendez may be identical twins, but there was no mistaking which brother stood to my right.

They were both strikingly handsome. Their shoulder-length chestnut curls and scruffy facial hair were synonymous with their identities at this point. Fox was the only one who took advantage of that, though.

In the off-season, he walked the runway at New York's Fashion Week. The photos of his black-and-white Calvin Klein shoot had all but broken the Internet, and you couldn't turn on the TV without seeing his Dior commercial.

However, when it came to Lynx Mendez, if he wasn't in his Bluecoats uniform, he was often spotted in a worn leather jacket, combat boots, and ripped jeans. The only time you saw his face on TV was on game days. Even his social media rarely showcased him. Something I decided was a damn shame as he took my hand in his own.

"I had the pleasure of enjoying some of your abuela's tamales a few days ago." He smiled warmly. "They were the closest I've had to my own abuelita's since we lost her four years ago."

Pride swelled through me as I graciously accepted the compliment on Abuela's behalf. "I know that, even more than hearing you liked the tamales, my abuela will be over the moon to know they made you feel closer to your abuelita."

As he withdrew his hand, Lynx studied me with narrowed eyes.

"Is everything okay?" I asked, breaking the silence that settled between us.

"He'll probably kill me if I told you this, but my man Jake's been talking about you nonstop for the last few days. I kind of feel like I already know you." He chuckled as he shifted his body weight from one side to the other. "I was trying to figure out if the version of Isa standing in front of me and the one he wouldn't shut up about were the same human."

"Jake's been talking about me?" The words flew out of my mouth without hesitation.

Instant regret trickled in as Lynx's eyes widened in curiosity. I should have continued the conversation by bringing up my father. Or, football in general. The weather. Why the sky was blue and the grass was green. *Anything other than Jake.* "Sorry. You don't have to answer that."

"You didn't hear this from me, but something about the girl that got away?" Lynx smirked.

There was a mischievous twinkle in the pools of his honey-brown eyes. If I didn't know better, I would think Lynx Mendez was standing here taking on the role of Cupid right now.

Casually, to get my attention with subtlety, he tilted his head forward. The simple motion was just enough to silently signal Jake's impending return to the bar area.

This time, however, Jake was joined by my brother. I couldn't read either of them. The uncertainty of what walked toward me gave me paralyzing panic.

With every step they took, I attempted to steady my breathing. The more I tried, the harder it became to focus on anything else.

You are a grown woman. A strong, independent, grown-ass woman. Pull yourself together, Isabel.

Just before Jake and Javier got to us, Lynx offered me a half-smirk and a wave. "It was nice meeting you, Isa. I'm sure I'll be seeing you around."

Before I had the chance to say any kind of goodbye, my older brother pulled me away.

"You're done for the night, Isa." The stern tone in Javier's voice sent a jolt of concern coursing through me.

In my entire life, he'd never talked to me like that, like I was a child in need of a lecture. And, while there were six years between us, Javier never treated me like I was his kid sister. Especially not at work.

"Don't worry, you're still getting paid for the night. Jake made damn sure of that." The hard lines on Javier's face dissipated as a slight grin spread across his lips. Leaning in, he lowered his voice drastically before adding, "Not everyone gets a second chance, sis. Make sure you take it."

Without elaborating, he loudly excused himself to "plan the Mendez Dirty Thirty." He turned on his heels but looked back, quickly pointing to where Jake was waiting.

Dumbfounded by the entire situation, I stood frozen in place like a deer in headlights as my brother continued to walk away.

For the second time that day, I had no words for what was happening to me.

Until it dawned on me

This whole thing was a fucking setup.

My brother knew Jake was going to be there early. He knew I wouldn't be needed on the floor all night because the Bluecoats in the house were just the Mendez twins and Jake.

There very well could be a thirtieth birthday being planned here, but Jake sure as fuck didn't need to be here for any of this.

And neither did I.

As if he could see me connecting the dots, Jake made his way over to me. "Please, don't be mad at your brother," he started. "This was all on me."

Rubbing my temples, my chest expanded as I took in a deep breath. I closed my eyes, sucking in air. On the exhale, I opened my eyes, unsure what I'd find upon doing so.

However, Jake Pierce with big puppy dog eyes that begged for forgiveness certainly was not it.

"And...what exactly is this?" I asked.

"Are you thirsty?" he replied, not even acknowledging my question. "Because I could *really* go for some fresh lemonade. The kind you can only get in Fox Hollow."

Bluecoats didn't belong to us exclusively, we took pride in them like they were our own. Football was everything.

Growing up, playing Pop Warner football was almost a rite of passage. Making the middle school team determined whether or not you continued your journey with the sport, and being part of the varsity team all but secured your college acceptance.

It was so cliché, but football was my first love. Nothing meant more to me. Isabel Coleman came pretty damn close, though.

Which was why, when I returned to Massachusetts last season, my first reaction was *"fuck yes!"* immediately followed by an *"ohhh shit."*

I knew there was no way I would be able to avoid her forever. Especially when the Colemans were the closest thing I had to family in Massachusetts now. It was why I bought the house I did without even looking at it. All I needed to know was it was on the same street Coach lived on. Anything else could be dealt with later.

After I found out I'd been traded, my mom decided to stay in Florida. She said the year-round sunshine was *"good for her soul."* Almost a year had gone by, and I missed the hell out of her. But for once, she was doing something for herself. She deserved it.

When I first moved back, I went to the practice facility and the stadium for game days. The only traveling I did was with the team. I avoided the grocery store. I turned my basement into a home gym. My trainer came to me. Getting swept up in celebrating my homecoming wasn't an option.

Within a few weeks of the season ending, I packed a couple of suitcases and headed to Fox and Lynx's family compo   ̀ n Montana. We were joined by Bluecoats tight ends: Ty As ̀ Benji Scott, and backup quarterback: Julian Teller. F arranged for the best coaches in the country to ͼ knowledge with us. Which included a week of me getting coached by Roger Coleman—again.

When Coach was there, the guys realized my relationship with him went well beyond one of former player and coach. It didn't take them very long to figure out Isa was much more than an old friend from high school.

By the time we returned to Fox Hollow in June, not only were we completely in tune with one another as football players, we were family.

For the first time since Isa broke my heart, I let people in.

For the first time since then, I didn't feel so alone.

Fox and Lynx were the ones that helped me come up with a plan to run into Isa. Neither of them would leave my house until I called Javier, who was in without hesitation.

Had I thought the whole thing through, I would have realized if I was genuinely trying to get closure—*if* I was genuinely over her—there'd be no need for a premeditated plan to move on. I would have already done it. It wouldn't matter if I saw her or not. The thought of running into her at the grocery store or seeing her at her parents' house if I dropped by wouldn't absolutely terrify me.

Of course, that epiphany moment didn't come until I saw her.

The sinking feeling of regret filled me as soon as the opening guitar riff of "What's My Age Again?" started.

I was the *"little birdie"* who told the DJ that blink-182 was Isa's favorite band. And, I was sure they still were because I checked her social media more often than I'd be willing to admit. Because of that, I knew she went to New Jersey last month to see them play at Warped Tour.

In hindsight, obsessively creeping on her Instagram was probably another clear indicator I was *definitely* nowhere near over her.

I silently watched her raise her fist in the air as she shook her hips back and forth. It was just as mesmerizing as it'd been when I took her to see the band live when we were sixteen.

Even from the back of the room of Retro where I was hiding in the shadows as the music played, I could feel her energy.

She froze as soon as she saw me. All emotion drained from her face. A stomach twisting panic filled me.

Abort. Abort. Abort.

It was too late, though. *No turning back now.*

Despite feeling like the world had been tilted on its axis and was spinning faster and faster by the moment, I did my best to keep my composure.

That lasted all of two minutes.

And now, we were in my truck.

I wasn't sure she would say yes. Honestly, I wasn't sure if I even wanted her to. But eventually, she did say yes.

Apparently, a Retro employee leaked the info that Fox, Lynx, and I were in the club. A small crowd had gathered outside of it. Fox and Lynx took one for the team and went out to take photos as Isa and I snuck out the back door.

As we made our way to the parking garage a few blocks away, I kept my head down. No one cared who I was in Montana, so I thought going out in public in Massachusetts wasn't going to be as big of a deal as the guys from the team made it out to be. I learned real quick that hats and sunglasses were now must-have wardrobe staples.

Normally, I didn't mind snapping a quick selfie or signing whatever it was that fans shoved in my face. However, people tended to forget I was human—just another person. I'd seen players' careers fall to the wayside after being rude to fans. As much as we said was about the game, the persona attached to the player was important.

My one and only concern was getting Isa out of there before someone noticed us. On instinct, I grabbed her hand when we dipped into the city streets. I apologized immediately and let go, but the small curl of her lips when I shrugged and made the excuse that "*old habits die hard*" gave me the tiniest sliver of hope.

After twenty minutes of driving in awkward silence, Isa made a comment about the weather. I tried my best to keep my eyes on the highway ahead of us, but I couldn't help but notice her shifting in her seat as she picked at her cuticles.

Thanks to the history we shared, I knew she was fidgety when nervous.

Me too, Bug. Me fucking too.

"So, are you still taking photographs for the football team?" I asked, desperate to keep the conversation going between us. As soon as the words left my mouth, I immediately wished I could take them back and ask about something else.

We graduated high school six years ago. Of course she wasn't hanging around the field at three o'clock in the afternoon, taking photos of the high school football team.

"No." Isa chuckled. "Having my own clients and working at Retro makes it hard. When I do go to games, I stay up in the bleachers with Mom and Abuela."

"That's too bad." Seeing a small window of opportunity opening, I decided to take it. "I'm going to stop by during varsity practice tomorrow. I wanted to see if you would take some pictures for me to put on my social media. You know, going back to where it all started."

Before she could answer, I clarified that I didn't expect her to do it for free. "I'll pay you, of course."

I didn't want her to think I had some kind of ulterior motive. I knew from a few friends I had made over the years in the industry that people seemed to have this idea that a photographer's time was free. But I'd seen firsthand how much time and effort went into producing the perfect photo.

I never wanted to be *that guy*. No matter my career status or how much money I had in the bank, *no one* owed me anything—least of all, Isa.

"Shut up. You will not!" She scoffed while letting out a laugh. It was the first unguarded glimpse of her that night, and I reveled in the sound. "I'll be there."

It was my turn to shift in my seat uncomfortably when I realized there were no more *safe* things to talk about. Which meant it was time to have the hard conversation. "So, we should probably talk about the elephant in the room..."

"Probably," she agreed, sighing. "And, I guess that probably means I owe you a little bit more of an explanation."

"That would be nice." I laughed as I pulled off the highway.

By the time we got to the old, flashing-yellow traffic light across the street from the exit, Isa began to tell me what happened after I left her backyard six years ago.

"It took my dad threatening to call the police for Devon to leave," she explained. "He was so angry. He punched a hole in the wall in the front foyer. You can still see the patch if you look close enough. As soon as he left, I called Salem. I didn't know he went to Kelsie's party, and I sure as hell didn't know he was telling people we had sex that night. We didn't. Not that night or any other night."

I don't tell her I'd been so angry that night I could have punched a wall myself.

When Devon came to that party, bragging about how he "*fucked Coach Coleman's daughter in his own house*," it took every ounce of restraint I had not to put *him* through a damn wall.

Not because I was jealous. Don't get me wrong, I *was* jealous, but Isa had been hell-bent on staying a virgin until she was married. More than anything else, I was disappointed at her for leaving her principles in the dust for a douche like Devon.

"I shouldn't have shut you out," she continued. Her voice shook as she apologized again. "I should have told you I just needed time. It all happened so fast and was just so much to wrap my head around. You deserved better, and I'm sorry."

In that moment, none of it mattered anymore. I just wanted to reach over and pull her into my arms—tell her it was okay. Deep down, I knew it wouldn't take much for me to forgive her. Now that I knew the truth of what happened, all I wanted to do was move forward.

Pulling over onto a dirt patch on the side of the road, I parked the car. The Sunnycrest Farm stand had been in the same spot for as long as I could remember. Every summer, someone from the farm came daily to refill the produce and restock the plastic cooler with ice, fresh lemonade, and iced tea. There was a drop box for cash and checks. The only thing that'd changed since I came here with my mom to get corn on the cob as a kid was the sign, now with the farm's PayPal and Venmo information on it to give people the option to digitally pay for their food.

Turning to face Isa, I sighed. *My turn.* "I'm sorry too." I shook my head as she opened her mouth. "I'm the one that put pressure on you to break up with Devon. I shouldn't have kissed you in the first place."

ISA

Jake's words played back over and over in my head as we walked up to the farm stand.

I pulled out my phone to pay for the lemonades and added an extra ten dollars for the watermelon I intended to take. I stopped by here just a few days ago to get flowers on the way to see my parents, so the farm's information was at the top of my recent purchases in the app.

While Jake reached down to open the cover of the big plastic cooler, I looked through the almost-empty wooden shelves for the pre-packaged watermelon slices I saw earlier in the week. There were assorted berries, vegetables, spices, and even freshly cut flowers, but no watermelon.

Jake grinned, holding up two glass bottles of lemonade. The water from the melting ice in the cooler dripped from the bottles as he made his way over to me. "Looking for anything in particular?" he asked.

Before I could answer, the sound of crunching gravel behind us stole our attention. At the sight of a hunter-green minivan pulling up behind Jake's truck, I laughed. With raised eyebrows, Jake turned to me for an explanation.

Sure, there were plenty of other hunter-green minivans in Fox Hollow. After all, I was fairly certain this town was the central hub for suburban football moms. Though, I was also quite sure there was only *one* mother in town that listened to nineties hip-hop on full blast in hers.

"I'm pretty sure it's Salem," I explained, still laughing.

Sure enough, before the door was even fully open, I heard her high-pitched squeal. Stepping out of the van in a pair of ripped denim shorts and a navy-stripe swing tank, Salem clapped excitedly as she waited for the back passenger door to slide open.

She dipped her body into the vehicle for just a moment. When she emerged, she was joined by a smaller redhead—her three-year-old son, Finnegan.

"Tia!!!!" he exclaimed as he ran toward me.

As I scooped him into my arms, I felt some of the tension that had settled in my shoulders loosen. It's amazing what a hug from an adoring toddler can do to one's state of mind.

I hadn't gotten the chance to text Salem to update her. For all she knew, I was still at Retro.

"Well, *this* looks like trouble," she mused, beaming as she opened her arms. "Listen, I don't care how many Super Bowl rings you have, superstar. Hug me, damn it."

The whining demand would probably be obnoxious if it came from anyone else on this entire earth. Somehow, Salem made it endearing.

It didn't surprise me that she knew just how to approach us. She'd always been good at reading a room. It was one of the reasons she made such an amazing preschool teacher.

Well, that, and her never-ending patience for small children.

I loved my nephew—her son—more than life itself, and I wanted kids of my own one day. But despite that, I knew I didn't have what it took to be in a classroom with four-year-olds all day and then go home and *mom* the heck out of a three-year-old. By yourself, nonetheless.

One thing I knew for sure: Salem O'Sullivan was a badass.

"Takes trouble to know trouble," Jake shot back playfully, before pulling her into a hug. "Hi, Salem."

With Finn secured safely in my arms, Salem grabbed a container of blueberries. After pulling out a small stack of cash, she pushed it down into the slot at the top of the box labeled "Cash & Checks."

"I have the day off tomorrow, so, I promised Finn pancakes," she started. "And we all know you can't have pancakes without blueberries from Sunnycrest. But, you know what would make my day off even better? If Tia Izzy came over in the morning," she hinted, not so subtly. "I always make enough to feed a small army, so you're more than welcome to come by too, Jake."

I expected Jake to make some sort of excuse. With training camp starting in the next couple of days, I would assume buttery pancakes covered in maple syrup weren't exactly his go-to breakfast right now.

"I have to meet my trainer for a session at one, but I can come by for a bit before that."

I tried my best to mask my surprise as Jake accepted her invitation.

I should have made some sort of excuse. Unlike the incident with the club, I could see this was a setup from a mile away. But she just *had* to go and throw Finn into the equation, knowing damn well I couldn't say no when it came to my favorite fella.

"I'll be there," I said.

JAKE

After Salem said her goodbyes, I placed the lemonades on an almost-empty shelf in the farm stand. I stopped when a bouquet of sunflowers wrapped in twine caught my eye. If my memory served me right, sunflowers were Isa's favorite.

"I already paid for the lemonade." Isa smiled. "And for the watermelon they didn't have. It'll probably cover the flowers, too."

"Like hell I'm going to let you pay for your own flowers."

Her eyes widened with surprise as I handed them to her. "These are for me? I just assumed...well, actually, I didn't know who they were for, but I didn't think—"

"I mean, they are your favorite, right?" I asked as I picked up the lemonades again, hoping I remembered correctly.

"They are," she confirmed. "You didn't have to, Jake."

"You're right. I didn't *have* to." I grinned as I sent twenty-five dollars from my phone to the farm stand. "I wanted to."

I didn't even check to see how much the bouquet was before paying for them, but I chuckled to myself when I saw the sign that read: "Sunflower Bouquets - $10 Each" as we walked back to my truck. The smile on Isa's face was well worth blindly paying double the amount.

"I think it's safe to say there's only one place we should drink these," I began, opening the passenger side door for Isa.

With the flowers in one hand, she used the other to pull herself up into the front seat.

"Whatcha say, Bug? You in for a little adventure?"

"With you?" she said. "Always."

The flickering rays from the setting sun danced in her eyes when she turned back to face me. My stomach tightened as she nodded. Being around her again was easier than I thought it would be.

The original plan for tonight was to simply break the ice. I just wanted to make sure that when our paths crossed naturally for the first time, it wouldn't be painfully awkward. There were so many emotions to still work through, and I wasn't delusional enough to think we could just pick up where we left off six years ago.

Hearing her side of what happened gave me hope, though— something I didn't think was possible earlier in the evening. Now, all I had to do was keep myself in check.

It was easy to fall in love with her.

During a game of tag on the playground in kindergarten, I fell on the pavement. My legs shook as I stood up. Both of my palms and knees were covered in bloody scrapes.

The tears welled in my eyes, but I tried so damn hard not to cry.

Until the sweetest little voice next to me whispered, *"I'm going to act like I have a headache and feel dizzy and you're gonna help me walk to the nurse's office, okay?"*

I could still see her big brown eyes pooled with worry as she waited for me to agree. When we got to the nurse's office, she handed over the hall pass given to her by the recess monitor and explained why she lied.

In all the movies I'd seen and stories I'd been read up until that point, the hero was always the guy—a prince, a knight.

It was in that moment I learned that sometimes it was actually the pretty princess who saved the day. Isa Coleman was the hero of that story, and so many of our stories after that as well.

Our paths crossed often, as they do in a relatively small town. We were in the same class a few times in elementary school. I found myself sneaking glances at her across the cafeteria in middle school.

Like most kids, we found ourselves surrounded by people with similar interests. Naturally, I hung out with other athletes. Isa was creative. Her friends were writers, actors, and artists.

I spent my Saturday nights at the mall. Isa's were spent at the skate park. There wasn't anything that brought us together. Until high school.

And, that was all thanks to her dad.

Roger Coleman took a huge leap of faith in me. As my high school football coach, he took me into his home under the guise of going over strategy. I was the only freshman on the varsity team. He said he wanted to make sure I knew all the plays. At least that's the story he told the other coaches.

He did a good job of hiding it, but I knew it was because my mom called and asked him if there was anyone that could give me a ride home after practices. As a single mom, Ruth Pierce tried her damnedest to take care of things on her own. As an emergency room nurse, she was expected to be on time for her shifts. When she realized there was no way she could be in two places at once, she swallowed her pride and asked for help.

Coach Coleman not only kept his promise that he, personally, would make sure I made it home safe every night, he went well beyond that.

"Can I ask you something, son?" he started as we walked to his truck. *"What's for dinner tonight?"*

I shrugged. "I don't know. Probably frozen pizza. Maybe leftovers. Mom usually sleeps while I'm at school, so I just wing it when I get home."

"Have you ever had real tacos? I'm not talking about the fake crap you can get from a drive-thru..."

Coach and I had just walked in the door when Isa barreled down the stairs. Headphones on and skateboard in hand, she was completely oblivious. Coach tried to warn me. The words just simply didn't leave his mouth fast enough.

Her tiny little frame slamming into my backside was nothing compared to getting pulled down and sacked on the field. It was, however, enough to send Isa tumbling back right onto her ass. The memory of her eyes widening with embarrassment as she reluctantly reached for my extended hand still made me laugh to this day.

"You know what I was just thinking of?" I chuckled while I waited for the oncoming traffic to pass. "The first time I had dinner at your parents' house."

"Oh God." The groan of embarrassment that came from the seat next to me made me laugh. "Whyyyy?"

During the ten-minute drive, we reminisced like we were old friends catching up after not seeing each other for a while. Talking about our memories together—the good times we'd had—made any remaining tension seemingly dissipate.

"Do you remember the first time I convinced you to sneak into the bog?" she asked. "You were so scared we were going to get caught and you would get kicked off the football team."

"And your parents were worried about me being the bad influence!" I scoffed playfully as I pulled into the street that led to our final destination.

Fox Hollow was known for two things: football and cranberries.

The stadium sat on the east side of town. The cranberry bog took over fifty acres of the west side. The Arthur J. Fairgrounds Stadium was known by most people in town and NFL fans alike simply as "The Fairgrounds."

Which was not to be confused with the family that owned both the stadium and the Fairgrounds Cranberry Co.

The Fairgrounds family might be small in size, but they were undeniably the biggest success story of Fox Hollow.

Over time, a small family-run bog passed down from generation to generation expanded itself into one of the region's biggest cranberry distributors. Hugh Fairgrounds turned cranberries into a football legacy when he purchased the Bluecoats and their home stadium.

Thanks to Hugh, I was back home now. He could say it was smart for business, but I wasn't naïve enough to think my trade didn't originally stem from the personal connection I had to Fox Hollow.

His son Matt was one of my closest friends growing up. We played football together as kids, but Matt loved the game a different way than I did. He loved the business side of the sport. As soon as high school was over, so were Matt's days of playing.

As the new Director of Player Personnel, Matt was the first person to call me and congratulate me when the trade was official. He was also the person I texted while at the farm stand, asking if I could go sneak into the cranberry bog. I didn't even have to tell him who it was with.

Within a minute of me texting him, I got a response.

Matt: Haha yeah man. My dad's actually at the bog house with Aunt Lou. I'll let him know you'll be swinging through. Tell Isa I said hey.

As we pulled into the parking lot, Isa's words the first time she brought me here came flooding back.

"This is the place I go to when I feel lost. I come here and I feel safe. I find myself again. I don't know if the bog will do the same for you, but I figured if it works, I can share."

"I have a confession," I started when I saw Hugh's white Cadillac Escalade parked outside of The Bog House. I wanted to "sneak" in for the nostalgia. However, I knew I would have to at least say hello to the owner of the team I played for. "I may be here with permission."

A sigh of relief left Isa. "Don't get me wrong, I would sneak in. I just haven't since..."

Her open-ended sentence didn't need to be finished.

I couldn't bring myself to come back until now either.

"I know." I nodded in understanding. "We don't have to go in. It's just...someone once told me that the bog was where they went when they needed to find themselves." I shifted my body to face her. "And I don't know about you, Bug, but I've been feeling pretty fucking lost."

ISA

"Okay."

I wished I had something witty or more profound to say in response. That seemed to be the overall theme of this evening, though—Jake Pierce leaving me without words.

But, he was right.

This place meant so much to me. For years, it was my safe place. Until it became *our* safe place.

I was thirteen the first time I saw the bog. The Bog House had been open to the public since Hugh and Louisa Fairgrounds took it over in the early nineties. The bog—where the cranberries were harvested—was not.

Right in the middle of the October harvesting season, my eighth-grade science class took a field trip to Fairgrounds Cranberry Co.

Looking back, I imagine I was the only one in my class who listened to Louisa Fairgrounds as she walked us through the marshy wetlands. The process of flooding the beds and pumping hundreds of thousands of floating red berries fascinated me.

I'm not sure why I ran back there later that night. I was devastated. I was scared. I thought I was going to lose my mom to ovarian cancer. For the first and only time in my entire life, I screamed at my father. I called him a liar. Then, I ran as fast as my legs would carry me to the bog.

I didn't stop until I found the fallen tree. Louisa found me sobbing. She didn't say anything as she sat down next to me. Terrified that she was going to call the police on me for trespassing, I began to apologize and explained what brought me back to the bog.

For the rest of my life, I'll never forget the compassion in her eyes when she told me I was always welcome there. I imagined, more than anyone else, she understood how calming the quiet stillness was. And we never spoke of it again.

In all the times I saw her after that, Louisa never mentioned it. Not to me or my parents. No one ever questioned my presence on the old, downed tree any time after that either. Not when it was just me, or when I started bringing Jake with me three years later.

Which was why, when her eyes lit up at the sight of me and Jake now approaching, I didn't think anything of it.

Not until she gasped and squealed with excitement.

"You're back! Both of you! Together!" She sighed happily as she walked over to us, but she stopped short, her face falling as she assessed me and Jake. "Oh. Just shopping today? I imagine in those shoes you won't be headed out back to the bog."

Jake chuckled when he looked down and realized she was talking about *his* bright white Nikes. "I'm not worried about my shoes," he said, waving her off as he reached for one of the wicker baskets that customers used while shopping. "I figured we'd come in, say hi, grab a few things, and then head back. If that's okay?"

Before Louisa could give us an answer, the loud voice of Hugh Fairgrounds came from the second floor.

"All right, who let the riffraff into the store?" He laughed at his own joke as he made his way down the stairs, and I couldn't help but grin at my godfather.

In the football world, he was known as the owner of the five-time Super Bowl championship winning Boston Bluecoats. To the town of Fox Hollow, he was simply one half of Fairgrounds Cranberry Co. He was also my dad's best friend—a friendship that began when my father played for the Bluecoats himself.

They only had a few seasons together before my dad retired from professional football, but when Hugh's wife and my mom got pregnant just weeks apart, they found another reason to bond.

Especially when Matthew Fairgrounds was born a week late and I was born a week early—both on June thirteenth. My mom and dad were chosen as Matt's godparents, and his as mine.

For a long time, our parents would joke that it was fate we were put on the earth together. We didn't necessarily disagree with them. It certainly wasn't in the meant-to-be together kind of way, though—for either of us.

We found *that* out when we were fifteen, after being pushed to kiss each other during a game of truth or dare. The conversation that followed was both awkward and relieving.

"It takes riffraff to know riffraff!" I teased as Hugh joined me and Louisa at the center of the store.

Jake, just a few feet away, loaded cranberry scones into his basket.

"She's got you there, big bro." Louisa laughed as she returned to her place behind the counter.

There was no mistaking that Louisa and Hugh were siblings.

Both of them had the same vibrant silver hair. Their weather-beaten faces, worn from days of wading in the bog, showcased prominent crow's feet. The crooks in the middle of their thin noses and the bluish-gray color of their eyes were identical too.

"I was just about to head out when Matty texted me and said you two were stopping by." Hugh grinned as his arms opened for a hug and I obliged on cue. "But, now I'm not too sure why I stayed."

We continued to go back and forth until Jake brought the overflowing basket in his arms to the checkout counter.

Straight away, I noticed Louisa wasn't ringing anything up. Jake pulled out his wallet to pay and turned to talk to Hugh about something football related. I was too busy trying not to laugh as Louisa made faces at the two of them to pay attention to the conversation taking place between the two men.

Until Louisa was about halfway through emptying the basket, and Jake realized she wasn't ringing anything up. After he questioned her about it, a sly grin began to spread across Louisa's face.

"I'll make a deal with you," she said. "If you take a picture and post where you got all this, you can have it for free. It's a win-win."

"I would have paid *and* posted a picture," he countered, shaking his head.

"I know." At that, she looked at me and Jake. "You know, I was starting to get a little worried we'd never see you two make your way back here."

I knew I should respond, but the truth was, I didn't know until Jake and I were almost here if he and I would ever make our way back to the bog—together or alone.

When Jake's items were packed up, Louisa told us not to be strangers. Hugh rushed to the door to open it for Jake and his two armfuls' worth of paper bags.

Once Jake's arsenal of cranberry goodness was tucked safely

into the back of his truck, he locked the doors and turned to me. "You ready?" he asked.

Who knew what we'd find down in the bog.

Maybe our tree wouldn't be there.

Maybe it wouldn't give me the same security it did when I was younger.

Or...maybe it would.

Maybe being here, with Jake, would fill the void that'd been in my heart since he left for college.

Was I ready for any of that? *Absolutely not.*

So, I lied.

"Ready if you are."

JAKE

STEPPING in mud was unavoidable in the marshy wetlands behind the store. I had already accepted that my new white Nikes would wind up in the trash, but I'd forgotten just how deep the puddles could be after a few rainy days.

Looking back, then down at Isa's feet, I laughed. I got her here and there was no way we were going back. I wasn't about to let her ruin her shoes too, though.

"Hop on." I patted my shoulders, fighting a smile when her eyes went wide. "There's no reason for us to both ruin our shoes."

"Jake." Isa rolled her eyes. "We are twenty-four years old. You are not giving me a piggyback ride."

"Oh, okay. I get it." I nodded. "You either think I can't handle it—which is just insulting—or you're scared."

A mischievous grin formed on her lips as she shook her head. "Same ol' Jake. Trying to bait me into trouble."

"Trouble?" I laughed. "Who said anything about trouble? I'm just a guy trying to help a girl get to a fallen tree."

She tilted her head in response. The unimpressed look on her face gave me déjà vu. I'd been here. Many, many times before. I recognized her stance immediately. Isa didn't agree with me and was about to start a fight.

"You and I together are always trouble." Looking ahead, she sighed. "Maybe we should just go back."

"Huh, so you are scared," I noted. "Not of the mud, though."

"What are we even doing here, Jake?" she asked with crossed arms. "What is all of this about?"

Fuck. Okay. I wasn't expecting to have this conversation, but if she needed to know why I was here, what *this* was all about...so be it.

"All I know is it's been six years and I haven't been able to get you out of my head," I confessed. "I miss you, Isa. It's as simple as that. Do I think that things are instantly going to go back to the way they were? Absolutely not. But I'd like to see if we can find out."

"But, I—"

"Don't. Don't do that." I shook my head. "We were kids. We both did some things we'd take back or change if we could. I don't blame you. You shouldn't either."

As her arms fell, so did her defenses. "Is the piggyback offer still an option?"

Part of me hated that I knew her so well. Despite the time that had passed, her mannerisms were the same. Picking at her nails, the inability to look me in the eye...they were all telltale signs that she was nervous. The unlinking of her crossed arms was her version of a truce.

My stomach knotted at the hope in her eyes.

As if I could ever say no to her.

She was right. This was trouble. *We* were trouble.

ISA

"I thought you'd never ask."

The ear-to-ear grin that spread across Jake's face caused a ripple effect. First, my mouth went completely dry, and then my heart began to race.

Friends.

He wants to be friends.

You can do this, Isa.

At that, I almost laughed at myself. It was bullshit and I knew it.

The truth was, I had one regret in this life. Just one single regret. Losing Jake has caused me so many sleepless nights. I'd spent more time wishing I could change how things ended with us than I'd care to admit—even just to myself. The fact that he was here, right in front of my face, made it even harder to avoid all the things I'd been trying so hard to forget.

Somehow, I willed myself to walk over to him. When he turned his back to me, I swallowed and jumped up, securing my legs around his waist. Even with shoes on, I could feel the hardness of his abdomen underneath my heels. I'd seen enough magazine spreads to know he had a fifty-seven pack under that T-shirt.

Okay, maybe it wasn't quite *fifty-seven*, but it was definitely more than six.

When we were kids, he worked out a lot. He was always muscular, but not like this. Not to the point that I could feel his shoulder muscles.

Shoulder. Muscles.

Who even had bulging shoulder muscles?!

Professional football players that had access to personal

trainers and the best gym equipment money could buy—that was who.

"I got you, Bug." He laughed as he hitched his arms under my thighs. "Relax."

Why I thought he wouldn't be able to feel my rigid body when he was quite literally carrying it was beyond me.

"Sorry." I loosened my grip around his neck and allowed my legs to fall to Jake's side. "I'm, uh...scared of heights?"

"Okay, if you're going to lie," he started, "you might want to make sure it's not to someone who knows better."

"It's a new phobia?" Scrambling, I tried my best to recover.

"You're less than six feet from the ground, Isa," he deadpanned as he started to make his way into the marshland. "And if I remember correctly, you're only scared of two things."

"I've outgrown my fear of the dark!" I said defensively.

The childhood fear of mine followed me well into my early twenties. I forced myself to sleep in a pitch-black room and faced it head-on. Now, I couldn't sleep if there was any light in a room.

"And thunder?" He chuckled. "Still scared of the big booms?"

"Not all of us can be fearless, Jake." I smiled as Jake stopped in front of the fallen tree we had claimed as *ours*. I planted my feet onto the ground below and locked eyes with him. The only sound that surrounded us was a natural melody of chirping crickets and the croak of a lone frog.

"Is that what you think?" Jake's voice sounded unsure as we locked eyes. "That I'm fearless?"

"I mean, I know we haven't been in each other's lives in a while, but, yeah," I said. "The Jake I knew wasn't scared of anything."

He changed the subject as he sat down on remnants of an old pine tree. "It was crazy to bump into Salem, huh?"

For the next hour, we caught each other up on what occurred in each of our respective lives over the last six years. Neither of us brought up past relationships, which was fine by me. I didn't think he cared to know about the guys I dated, and I was thankful not to hear about the women lucky enough to spend time in his bed.

As the hues of oranges and pinks from the sunset began to shine through the trees, Jake stood up and extended his hand to me. "We should probably think about getting you home."

JAKE

I CURSED as I reached over to turn off the alarm on my nightstand. A second string of expletives left my lips when I realized my cock was as hard as a rock. A visit from Isa in my subconscious slumber wasn't a new occurrence. Having seen her in person provided a more vibrant vision for my mind to utilize, though.

Holding onto the image I had in my head before the droning buzz of my alarm ripped me from my dream, I began to slide my hand up and down, over my shaft. My grip tightened when I wondered if she thought of me when she pleasured herself. If she moaned while imagining my wanting mouth on her in lieu of her own delicate and talented fingers—the very ones that captured beauty in film, now capturing a sensual keepsake just for me. If her lips parted, thinking of mine worshipping her in the precise place I wanted to. The idea of tasting her and taking her over the edge pushed me right over my own.

"Fuuuuuuuck."

I hadn't thought of the repercussions of my climax beforehand. After taking a look around, I bent down to grab the T-shirt from last night laying on my floor. On my way to the shower, I tossed the T-shirt in the trash.

It was time to focus on the next dilemma.

What the hell is a guy supposed to wear to brunch?

ISA

I barely got any sleep and somehow still woke up feeling like Snow fucking White.

As soon as the front door was closed behind me last night, the doorbell rang.

When I opened the door, Jake handed me the lemonade we never drank and the flowers I had forgotten in his truck.

"I was just about to pull out of the driveway when I realized your flowers were in the backseat. And...we never drank our lemonades."

"Where's yours?" I asked, looking for the second bottle.

"In the truck still." He smiled knowingly. "I'll see you in the morning, Bug."

He was halfway down the front walkway when I called out, "Jake —wait!"

"Yessss?" He chuckled as he turned back around.

"Call me and let me know you made it home safe?"

And, he did.

What, in theory, should have been a quick and simple confirmation turned into a three-hour-and-seven-minute conversation.

And it probably would have lasted longer than that if I hadn't fallen asleep.

Waking up to the annoyance of my phone being at two percent was quickly overshadowed by the *"Sweet dreams, Bug"* text from Jake waiting for me on my lock screen.

We so easily slid back into our former selves. The versions of

Jake and Isa that never existed without each other. After spending the last six years convinced there was no way he would ever forgive me, I was still having a difficult time wrapping my head around last night.

Caffeine might help.

Quietly, I made my way up the stairs. Before I could worry about what I'd wear to brunch at Salem's, I needed tea.

As I filled the kettle with water, I lowly sang "Addicted" by Simple Plan. Halfway through the chorus, I twirled, stopping short when I saw my brother's fiancé standing in the doorway.

"Holy hell, Adam. You scared the crap out of me." My heart raced as I put the kettle I almost dropped to the floor on the stovetop. "What are you doing home? Are you feeling okay?"

Normally by this time, Adam was long gone for the day. My brother required more sleep than I did, so even after the nights I worked until two in the morning, I usually had the kitchen to myself for my first cup of tea.

"I didn't want to interrupt your jam sesh." He shrugged, joining me in the kitchen. "Javier didn't tell you? He's not the only one on vacation for the rest of the week," he hinted with a smile. "I didn't want to miss Abuela's birthday party."

That would make Abuela—and my mom—so glad.

Mom spent the last year planning Abuela's eightieth birthday. We were all hopeful Abuela was still completely oblivious to the surprise. No one had talked about it at my parents' house. Everything was discussed via email or text. Mom was even able to keep the secret that Abuela's sisters would be coming from Mexico for the festivities.

I knew it would mean a lot to Abuela to have Adam there too. Much like Jake had when we were younger, Adam secured his spot in our family incredibly early on. My dad even joked that if Javier and Adam ever broke up, he would exercise his parental rights to still see Adam.

"He didn't tell me, but I know that'll make Abuela happy. I still can't believe we've managed to keep this whole thing from her for a year."

"I know! I was sure Papa Coleman would have spilled the beans by now." Adam chuckled again, this time as he made his way to the cabinets that held the coffee mugs. "So, how was your night? Rumor has it you left Retro with a certain wide receiver..."

"Yeah. I'm sure you and Javi had nothing to do with that setup either." I turned, narrowing my eyes in his direction.

The smirk on his face gave him away. "I don't know what you're talking about, sis."

"And you're a terrible liar, *bruh*."

"Okay, *but*, I need to know if you and Jake finally cleared the air after all those years of regret and wishing you both hadn't fucked up?" His back was to me as he looked for his favorite coffee mug.

When he turned to face me, the old Cape Cod mug in hand, I reciprocated the knowing smile that lit up his face.

"I didn't realize you knew so much about me and Jake's history." I laughed. "But, yeah. That about sums it up."

"In all the years I've known you, I've seen you drunk *one* time," he said, not needing to clarify it was the night I saw a photograph posted on Jake's Facebook of him kissing another girl. "And when we—you know, everyone but you—went down to Miami for Jake's first game as a Dolphin, we met up with Jake and his mom for dinner one night. All he could do was talk about you. It doesn't take a genius to connect the dots."

Over two cups of tea (for me) and coffee (for Adam), I relayed what happened last night. Once Adam was caught up, I stood up to wash my mug out. I loved getting to spend time with Adam. We didn't get much time together, just the two of us. However, I still needed to figure out what I was going to wear to Salem's.

"So, what are you wearing to brunch?" Adam asked as if he were reading my mind. "You know I adore you and your style, but can I recommend shoes that aren't Converse and maybe pants that don't have rips all over them?"

"How about you just come down to the Bat Cave and help me pick something out?" I suggested, referring to my section of the house by the nickname he'd given it shortly after I moved in.

"I'd love to!" He smirked. "And while we decide what you'll wear, we can go back to discussing Jake's muscles. Don't think I didn't catch you stopping yourself from dishing about them."

JAKE

I HOPED I would beat Isa here.

Salem still lived in the same house she grew up in—which was only two streets over from me now. I *hoped* I would beat Isa here... but I should have known I wouldn't.

As I parked behind her Jeep, I took a second to brace myself. Salem had been forgiving last night, but it very well could have been a fleeting moment. She was Isa's strongest ally. The two of them were a package deal. They always had been. Which meant that it was just as important for me to mend the bridge with Salem as it was for me to fix things with Isa.

Isa and Salem were thick as thieves growing up. While Isa and I may have considered each other best friends, I knew I was actually the runner-up in that department. Where you found one of them, the other wasn't too far behind. They did everything together. The little interaction we had last night told me not much had changed between the two of them over the years.

Which meant this brunch was so much more than a few old friends catching up. This was the tryout of all tryouts. Even though we all knew one another, there was no doubt in my mind that Salem O'Sullivan was trying to make sure I was still good enough for her best friend.

With that in mind, I rang the doorbell.

Don't fuck this up, Jake.

After the longest minute of my life, the front door swung open.

After last night, there was no pretending any feelings I had for Isa were platonic.

I never stood a chance.

Something that was confirmed the second she beamed at my presence on the front porch.

Her gorgeous, dark auburn curls that were pulled up and away from her face last night, now fell down around her shoulders. The intricate Mexican candy skull tattoo on her left upper arm was now on full display. As I scanned over her body and admired how the black fabric of her bodysuit hugged her curves, I was thankful I decided to wear a white button-up shirt and black slim-fitting slacks.

Funny enough, when I looked through my closet, Isa's father's voice rang in my head.

"It's always better to be overdressed than underdressed, son."

Roger Coleman was the closest thing I ever had to a father of my own.

Stefano Moretti—the man half-responsible for my very existence—denied me until the day I made national headlines for winning the Heisman Trophy. Intuition told me to stay far away, but there were so many things I wanted answers to. So, I agreed to meet him for lunch.

The first strike was when he tried to justify his absence with the excuse that my mother tried to trap him with her pregnancy. Then, he continued to make excuses for why he didn't show up any time after that. The only consistent thing about his bullshit was it was never his fault for being a deadbeat parent.

"Don't forget about your old man if you get signed" was the second strike.

Those were the words he left me with before we parted ways. We hadn't seen each other since. Before I left the restaurant parking lot, I blocked his phone number.

Any chance of him building a relationship with me was gone when he took it upon himself to fabricate a story about my mom keeping me from him and how devastated he was that he missed out on my childhood.

Strike Three.

The media ate that shit up like candy. My agent and his team handled most of the backlash and strongly encouraged me to let it just *"blow over."* I couldn't, though.

Stefano gave me nothing. Not even his time. I owed him nothing. My mother deserved all the recognition. Roger Coleman earned the right to be acknowledged for stepping into shoes he never asked to wear.

So, I told the truth. Including the story of how Coach Coleman took me shopping for my first press conference outfit. Seventeen-year-old Jake thought a tie wasn't necessary; Coach insisted. I never forgot the advice he gave me that afternoon.

In fact, it was that very advice that played back in my head as I decided what to wear today.

"Mornin', Jake."

The way my heart began to race at Isa's smile brought me back to standing on her parents' front porch before our junior prom. Coach had been so relieved when he found out we were going together. I had friend-zoned myself to the point that even her overprotective father wasn't fazed by my presence anymore.

But even though Coach Coleman wasn't worried about his precious—and *only*—daughter being out with me...I was.

I was forever worrying I'd slip up, cross the line, and ruin everything. That was never an option. Our friendship meant too much to me. Isa meant too much to me.

Her parents insisted on paying for everything—the stretch Hummer we all rode in, the pre-prom photographer, even my tuxedo. My mom had been so worried about looking like she was accepting charity. It only took one lunch with Alma Coleman for her to realize the Colemans were simply good people.

"Are you going to come in?" Isa laughed as she stepped back from the doorway.

"Yeah, sorry." I chuckled. "I was just thinking about junior prom and the summer after it."

Her eyebrows raised in wonder, but she didn't say anything as she led me to the bright, open kitchen.

I tried my damnedest to keep my eyes up. I really did. But as her hips sashayed back and forth, the desire to be a gentleman quickly dissipated. Instead, I found myself wishing I were in a position to grab her ass.

When we were younger, I decided Isa had the perfect butt. I wasn't disappointed to see it held true to this day.

As we entered the kitchen, my stomach tightened.

"Look, Finn," Salem said, smiling brightly, "Mr. Jake brought you flowers!"

"I sure did." I grinned in return when the little redhead by her side eyed me warily.

The flowers were bought with Salem in mind, but I went along with it. I knew a setup when I saw one. It was also why I agreed to brunch today. Salem was up to something. I wasn't sure what, but I wanted to find out. Curiosity killed the cat, after all.

"I was just telling Finn that it's totally cool for girls to play with trucks," she said before her smile turned into a tight line. "We had a moment in school yesterday. So, it's kind of perfect you brought these flowers for him, Mr. Jake."

"Red's my favorite color!" Finn noted as he looked at the autumn bouquet. The vibrant red roses stuck out in the midst of the yellows and oranges of the other flowers. "Fanks, Mr. Jake."

"Sure, little man," I replied, smirking at him.

Salem opened the fridge, reached in, and then handed a sippy cup full of milk to Finn. Facing Isa, she continued. "Why don't you get Jake something to drink and then meet us in the dining room?" She didn't wait for a response before she turned to Finn. "You ready for some pancakes, bubs?"

Isa's eyes narrowed in warning. It wasn't about getting me a drink. There was a hidden message laced in Salem's words. One I couldn't easily find. Then again, the two of them always had entire conversations I never seemed to be a part of.

Which was how I *knew* they were no longer talking about a drink at all when Isa said, "Sure thing, Salem. I'll get right on that."

Salem's eyes sparkled, her lips turning up as she looked at the two of us. "Oh, I'm sure you will."

ISA

I WAS GOING to fucking kill her.

Twenty years of friendship were about to end in homicide because Salem just couldn't help but stir the damn pot.

I made the mistake of coming early—giving my best friend just enough time to figure out I was harboring *something* for Jake. What exactly that was, I still wasn't sure of myself. That didn't stop Salem, though.

"You know I've always been Team Jasa."

"Team Jasa?" I repeated. *"What the hell is a Jasa?"*

"You and Jake—Jake. And. Isa—Jasa."

"Orange juice?" I asked, not bothering with any of the other options in Salem's fridge. "There's a gallon of extra pulp."

While most people didn't seem to prefer orange juice with the pulp—never mind *extra* pulp—everyone in my family loved it.

Shortly after he'd started coming by for dinners, Jake started going out of his way to stop by the house to walk with me to school in the mornings.

After a couple of weeks, my mother insisted he come eat breakfast with us. Most mornings, it was simple—cereal, toaster pastries, frozen waffles, a granola bar on the go—but every Monday, my mom went crazy.

My dad always said there was no way anyone could have a bad week after having one of Mama's breakfasts.

Huevos, rancheros, beans, chorizo, salsa, handmade tortillas, green or red chilaquiles... she chose the options depending on her particular mood, but the one thing that stayed the same was that Javier and I would both have a big glass of cold orange juice. Mom apologized for what felt like a hundred times when she realized Jake probably wouldn't drink the orange juice, but he took a glass anyway.

As it turned out, he loved it. He couldn't stop reveling in how much better it was than the pulp-free orange juice he'd been drinking his entire life. Before we left for school, he drank three full glasses. After that, my mom always made sure to have *extra* orange juice for our Monday breakfasts.

Since then, I thought of him every single time I had a glass of orange juice.

It was something so insignificant. So small.

But, there were a million more little memories like that as far as Jake was concerned.

"Please." His smile was small. Unsure.

Shit. Should I have offered him something else? What if he didn't like orange juice anymore and he was just being polite?

"So..." Jake shifted his body as his eyes found mine. "I know it's last minute, but with the season starting soon, my life is about to get crazy. Any chance you're free tomorrow after four? I can make dinner?"

"You cook?" I teased as I grabbed the container of orange juice from the fridge.

"Okay, fine, I'll probably order something," he admitted, laughing. "What do you say, Bug?"

JAKE

I wasn't sure where those words came from.

I certainly didn't walk through Salem's front door thinking I would ask Isa to come to my house. For dinner. Like, a date.

Shit. Should I clarify that it wouldn't be a date? I mean, unless she wanted it to be. No, Jake. Not a date. Chill out, man.

"How about five?" Isa handed me the glass of orange juice, looking at me expectantly as she awaited my answer. "Does that work?"

"Five is perfect," I told her as I took the glass from her hand. It would give me enough time to get my workout out of the way, shower, and plan something for dinner.

I lowered my voice before I said, "Do you think it would be lame if I invited Salem and Finn to training camp tomorrow? There will be family-friendly activities all over...well, you know."

Isa practically grew up in that stadium. She was too little to remember her dad playing, but as soon as she discovered her love for football, Coach Coleman took her to every single Bluecoats home game.

She knew her shit, too. She could call plays better than most of the refs and talk player stats all day long. She knew just as much about the game as I did. Maybe even a bit more. It was one of the reasons I fell in love with her.

"Only if you don't invite me too." She shrugged nonchalantly. The hopeful sparkle in her eyes conflicted with the standoffish stance she tried to play off. "I know that's a lot of me for one day, but selfishly, I really wanna go."

"You want to come to training camp?" I questioned. I'm not sure why the notion surprised me. It shouldn't. "I was given tent passes for tomorrow's camp. So, you wouldn't have to sit in the sun, and you'd have access to the bathrooms in the field house."

Training camp was open to the general public. There were a few tents off to the side for players' families and "*distinguished guests*"—which basically meant whatever celebrities decided to pop by for the day. Despite the fact that I insisted I didn't need any, ten passes were left for me on my locker shelf anyway.

Matt's messy handwriting across the envelope read, "*Welcome home, Pierce!*"

I left practice that day and went right to the Colemans' house. I left three passes with Coach Coleman, Mama Alma, and Abuela. Yesterday, when I saw Javier, I gave him two passes, for him and Adam.

"Of course, I want to go." With that, she rolled her eyes dramatically.

"Well, you'll be in good company. Abuela, your parents, Javi, and Adam are all going too." The thought of having all the Colemans on the field, even just for training camp, left me with the most content feeling. It was like the universe finally settled as it should, that things were finally all aligned. "Oh, speaking of Abuela...I'm going to need your help with her gift."

"Are you going on Saturday? I assumed with camp starting you wouldn't make it."

"Camp ends at one. I'll leave the stadium by three. That gives me plenty of time to shower and make it to your parents' house by seven," I rattled off. "There just won't be too much eating or drinking."

"Well, we should probably head into the dining room before Salem comes out and insinuates that we were—*never mind.*" Her cheeks flushed as she stopped herself from completing her sentence. "We should just go in there."

Oh, hellllllllllll no.

"Nope. No way. Finish it, Isabel." I laughed softly, and Isa's face scrunched in confusion when I called her by her full name. "What would Salem insinuate?"

Much like when she called me *Jacob*, I only used her full name when situations held a certain...*je ne sais quoi.*

Like right now, for example, when I needed her to tell me what her best friend would insinuate. By the looks of Isa's pink rosy cheeks and her inability to look me in the eye, there wasn't a single doubt in my mind it was something sexual.

Six years ago, I would have let it go. Younger Jake would've just dropped it if the conversation started to head toward that unknown territory. But if nothing else, the last six years without Isa taught me there was no better time like the present. Time waited for no one.

And sure enough, Isa mumbled something about '*sex*' and '*ridiculous*.' Her thumb picked at the cuticle of one of the nails on her other hand as she swallowed.

"I'm sorry, what was that? You're going to have to speak up, Isa. I can't hear you."

"You're such an ass, Jacob Pierce." The glare in her eyes when she finally looked at me was the cutest thing I'd seen in my whole life. "You know damn well what I said."

"Fine. You're right." I grinned, leaning in as if I were about to tell her a secret. "I know what you said—what you meant—but, just for the record, I don't think the idea is *ridiculous*."

ISA

WITHOUT ANOTHER WORD, or time for me to offer a rebuttal, Jake left me in the kitchen. Not that I would have had much to say, anyway.

What did he mean that he didn't think it was ridiculous?

Did he just imply that he wanted to have sex with me?

Holy shit. He did. He definitely did.

Because the conversation Salem had not so covertly referenced was the one we were mid-having as Jake showed up. The one where she was trying to convince me to *"at the very least, find out if he fucks with as much intensity as he plays football."*

After regaining control of my senses, I joined everyone in the dining room.

The only one that seemed to notice me was Finn—a syrup-covered toddler. In the few minutes it took for me to get my shit together, Salem and Jake had managed to start an intense conversation about the potential of a Super Bowl repeat in the upcoming season.

"Wook, Tia." Finn grinned as he pointed at the plate full of pancakes, bacon, and scrambled eggs in front of him. "Momma made me *special* Mickey Mouse pancakes!"

I smiled back at him before answering how cool that was. I was the closest thing Finn had to an aunt. When Salem's parents retired, they bought an RV—and they'd been traveling across the country since. Without any siblings or cousins nearby, *my* family was her family.

Salem's dad came back to visit and check on the house every few months. Whenever he did, he'd always insisted that Salem go out. So, in between those visits, it was often me or even *my mom* that got a phone call, asking if we could watch Finn so Salem could run errands or go to doctor's appointments.

There was never a time we said no. We saw how hard it was for Salem. Finn's dad wasn't in the picture. She was raising this little boy all on her own. And she never complained. Not once.

We loved Finn, but it was Salem's sheer lack of expectation that made our family want to help her. There was never a time she didn't offer to pay us for babysitting. Of course, we always refused her money.

"Para eso estamos," my mom would tell her after getting the chance to spoil Finn for the day—meaning that was just what family did. "We love you and our Finn."

Salem was my best friend, but my parents would move heaven and earth for both her and Finn. My mom usually cooked with Manteca, but once we found out Finn had a peanut allergy, she made sure to keep sunflower seed butter in the house just for him. They had toys at their house for him and floaties for the pool. *My* dad was the one that took time off from work when Salem needed emergency gallbladder surgery when Finn was just seven months old.

Things like that earned them their "Abuela" and "Papa" titles before Finn was even a year old. Abuela was absolutely thrilled to be promoted to Bisabuela. Maybe we didn't all share the same bloodline, but we were family.

"That settles it then," Jake said from across the table.

As our eyes connected, the intensity of our locked stare sent a shiver down my back. The small shudder of my body was just enough to blow any cover I may have had. The illusion that Jake wasn't affecting me was diminished in two seconds flat.

At that, Jake's lips turned upward into a knowing smirk.

Right before he broke the connection, he winked at me.

The motherfucker winked at me.

We were in trouble.

I was in trouble.

JAKE

Old habits definitely died hard.

As I turned to face Salem, Isa's stare felt like fire dancing on my skin.

I knew how to get under hers—how to get into her head—and I used that to my advantage in the kitchen.

Isa needed resolve. Leaving the room without explaining myself was strategically intentional. I *wanted* her to think about it. I wanted her to obsess over what I meant until it festered enough in her head that she couldn't contain it anymore.

Because then, she'd bring it up again.

It was childish. I'd admit that. I could have stayed in the room. We should have finished the conversation. There was something self-satisfying in knowing I was getting to her, though.

Watching her squirm in her seat and the growing flush in her cheeks when I winked at her only fed the flame.

Focus, Jake. There's plenty of time to harbor mixed emotions when it comes to Isa. Now is not the time or place.

When she moaned in satisfaction after taking a bite of a cinnamon coffee cake, I knew that focusing was out of the question.

"Salem..." she started. Her chest rose and fell as she sighed in satisfaction. "This coffee cake is delicious."

Salem thanked her and continued on about the process of making the perfect cinnamon swirl, all the while simultaneously breaking up more bacon for Finn.

I shifted in my seat, still watching Isa and trying my damnedest to ignore the twitch in my cock. Just like that, for the first time in my life, I was jealous of an inanimate object. Of food, nonetheless. If coffee cake could do that to her, I could only imagine what sounds might leave her lips in the throes of an orgasm.

My new life goal was to find out.

"You okay, Jake?" Salem asked.

"Oh, yeah." I grinned. "Just thinking about something *ridiculous.*" I zoned in on Isa and she nearly choked when her eyes widened.

Out of the corner of my eye, I saw Salem shake her head. "Okay, I'm definitely missing something. Someone better tell me what's going on."

"Absolutely not," Isa shot down quickly. Her eyes narrowed in my direction as if to warn me to keep my mouth shut.

Salem leaned in closer to me. "Come on. We can pretend to clean up while you tell me all the things Isa doesn't want me to know!" Turning to Finn, she smiled. "Tia will stay here with you while Mr. Jake and I start bringing the dirty dishes back to the kitchen. Why don't you tell her allll about Paw Patrol? I'm sure Tia would love to hear about Chase and Everest!"

"And Marshall!" Finn added happily.

"Yes," Salem agreed, as she stacked plates on top of each other. "Especially Marshall!"

I'd forgotten how much I missed this—being in their company.

Following her lead, I grabbed a few of the near-empty serving dishes on the table. Once we were in the kitchen and out of earshot, she turned back to face me.

"What are you doing, man?" she asked quietly. "As happy as I am to see you...coming around after six years? We might be older, but you're still the same. I can see what you're trying to do with Isa. Don't."

"I don't know what you're talking about."

Playing dumb wouldn't work. Not here. Not with Salem. She knew about my past with Isa. More than that, she was the only person who knew how I felt about Isa when we were kids.

Her raised eyebrows and the small snort of disbelief called me out immediately.

"Okay, fine," I conceded. "But, it's more than you think."

She flipped the lever on the kitchen faucet, not saying a word as she began to rinse off the dirty dishes.

"She's always been more than that to me, and you fucking know it." My voice was low, but there was no hiding the emotion packed in my defense.

"I just needed to hear you say it." She grinned as she wiped her hand on a kitchen towel. "So, what's the plan?"

ISA

INSTEAD OF GOING BACK HOME after brunch, I drove a few streets over to my parents' house. It seemed pointless to drive thirty minutes home just to drive thirty minutes back to Fox Hollow to take photos at the high school's football practice for Jake.

I didn't tell my mom or dad that I was coming by...*or about Jake.*

Knowing the front door was always unlocked during the day, I let myself in. I wandered around my childhood home—peeking in rooms as I went along—until I found Mom and Abuela in the kitchen.

The cinnamon lingering in the air when I walked in the door should have been a giveaway. Today was the first day of the varsity team's practice. Which meant one thing: Mom and Abuela were making polvorones for the team—classified as sweet bread but commonly known as cookies.

"I should have known," I chuckled, scooping a polvorón up as I passed by. "Yum pan dolce," I said, sighing with content as I took the first bite. The outside was crunchy with a nice crackly top, but the inside was soft and chewy. It tasted like magic. Perfectly baked magic. "Make sure you throw some extras in there for Jake. He'll be at practice tonight."

"Isabel!" Mom exclaimed, wiping her hands on her apron. An ear-to-ear grin greeted me as she pulled me into a hug. "I didn't know you were coming by today, mija."

"Bueno. Isabel can make las galletas ahora." Abuela chuckled as she took off her own apron and handed it to me. She planted a quick kiss on my cheek before she walked over to the kitchen sink to wash her hands. "¡Hola, Mariquita!

Neither of us could tell you why she chose to call me "Ladybug."

That didn't change the fact that it was one of my favorite nicknames. The older I got, the more I appreciated having something like that with my grandmother.

Even at almost eighty, Abuela was a spitfire.

Her aging body may have slowed her down a bit, but her mind was still sharp as a nail. So much that she only just agreed to move into my parents' house a year ago—and it took an incredible amount of convincing from my mom and dad. Even though she'd spent most of her time at our house growing up, she'd had her own townhouse as well. I couldn't imagine what it felt like giving up her independence after having it for so long.

One of five daughters, Evita Isabel Torres Velasquez fled to America in 1957 with nothing but a backseat full of baby clothes, a map, and five hundred dollars. She was eight months pregnant with my mother—desperate to get away from an abusive husband. She planned for months, saving and hiding money every chance she got. Her two older sisters helped her in any way they could. One of them got her the 1929 Ford Model A she drove across the border into Texas. Not long after that, she settled in Massachusetts and changed her name to Evita De la Rosa—paying homage to her childhood best friend and little sister Rosa.

From what I was told, my biological grandfather looked for her for years. In the stories she told, Abuela called him "El Diablo." When I was younger, I likened him to Voldemort (the dark wizard in Harry Potter). We didn't speak his name, and when we did talk about him...there was nothing good to be said.

She did whatever she needed to survive on her own. No matter how hard things got, returning to Mexico was never an option. She taught herself English and became a United States citizen on my mom's tenth birthday. She didn't contact anyone in her family until my mom turned eighteen—not until Abuela knew her husband couldn't come and take my mom away. Then, she filed for divorce.

I couldn't imagine not being able to drop in and see my mom and dad. And Abuela too. How hard it must have been for her to be all alone in a foreign country, how selfless she had to be to give up everything she'd ever known in order to ensure my mom's safety. She missed out on so much in life because she was always looking over her shoulder.

It'd never been lost on me that I got to live the life I have because my abuela was brave.

"¡Hola, Abuela!" I smiled, pulling the apron over my head. "Did you find anything good on Netflix?"

Last time I was over, I set her up with her own Netflix profile and showed her how to use it. She was over the moon when she saw they had so many of her favorite telenovelas, and quite a few she hadn't seen yet.

"¡Oh, si!"

Her eyes lit up as she started telling me about the shows she'd been watching. I made a mental note to watch a few of the ones she seemed really into. It would give us something to talk about the next time I came over.

When Abuela paused, Mom let out a chuckle. "Abuela has become quite the little binge-watcher."

Waving her off, Abuela made me promise to come say goodbye before I left and excused herself to go "*binge-watch*" La Reina del Flow.

Mom shook her head as she leaned in toward me. "I tried telling her I didn't need any help."

"Lo escuché!" Abuela called out and I burst out in laughter.

"So, Jake, huh?" Mom smirked without skipping a beat. "I heard you saw him last night."

"Oh, yeah? Did you?" I rolled my eyes. The only person she could have gotten that information from was my brother. "I'm sure Javi forgot to mention it was an ambush—partially set up by him."

"¡Basta!" she scolded as she scooped flour into the mixing bowl. "Your brother was just trying to help."

Arguing with her was pointless. My mom and I were close, but Javier was a mama's boy. My brother could very well murder someone and not only would my mom let him hide the body in her backyard, she'd also be his alibi. Javi could do no wrong in her eyes.

"And don't think changing the subject is going to get you off the hook, mija," she added, as she began to knead the dough in her hand. "It's about time you and Jake patched things up. All this over a silly little kiss when you were kids."

She was baiting me. She wanted me to admit it was more than just a "*silly little kiss.*" I never talked about what happened between me and Jake—not with my mom, at least.

Javier knew, though. I assumed some things were safe between the two of us, but by the way my mother was fishing right now...

"I know," I agreed, not wanting to give her any fuel to feed the fire.

Jake and I had only *just* found our way back into each other's lives. We didn't need an extra push from Alma Coleman.

Everything my mother did was done with the best intentions. However, it wasn't always executed properly. My mom could be pushy—especially if she felt strongly about something. I needed more time to figure out what I was feeling before she started trying to shove us back together.

"*You know?*" she repeated suspiciously. "That's it? No argument? Just, *you know?*"

"What do you want me to say, Mom?" I asked. "You're right. It's been long enough. It's time to put the past behind us."

"So, that's why you got all dressed up for brunch at Salem's?" she pushed. "Just to *put the past behind you?*"

Damn it, Javier.

"I don't know what Javier told you," I started as I transferred the treats from the cooling racks to the platters set out on the counter. "But, yes, I went to brunch at Salem's. Salem invited me and Jake when she saw us at the farm stand last night."

My mother stopped what she was doing and stared at me sternly. "Mírame a las ojos."

I paused at the warning in her tone—her statement. It was something she always said to me when she thought I was hiding something—*look me in the eye*—daring me to try to lie to her face again.

It was time to redirect the conversation. She wouldn't let this go; I knew that much. Between my mom and Salem this morning, I just needed a small break from the matchmaking attempts. "Is Dad here? I'm going to practice tonight to take photos, and I want to talk to him about a few things."

"Your father didn't mention anything about you going to practice."

Again, she was digging.

This time I was expecting it, though.

"I'm just doing a favor for an old friend."

JAKE

THE FIELD WAS EMPTY.

Practice wasn't expected to begin for another hour, but something told me I needed to get there early.

After my training session, I showered and made my way over to the place that had been my home away from home for four years of my life. I owed everything I had to my time here at Fox Hollow High School. If it weren't for Coach Coleman and the other coaches on the team teaching me the fundamentals of football and about work ethic in general, I wouldn't be in the NFL.

There were no days off, even in the off-season. If you weren't committed to playing another sport or school activity, you spent your time after school in the weight room. As we got older, things like after-school jobs were also taken into consideration.

Coach wasn't a tyrant by any means. Quite the opposite, really. If you didn't want to put the work in, he wouldn't force you; you just wouldn't be part of the starting lineup.

The summer before freshman year, the weight room opened up to students wanting to utilize what the school had. I was the only freshman that showed up every day—even on the weekends.

After two weekends in a row, Coach invited me to the varsity tryout. I made the team and started in the very first game. He was hard on me. Sometimes it felt like Coach pushed me harder than anyone else. But, man, it felt fucking good to make him proud. It still did.

That was all I ever wanted.

Well, that...and to date his daughter.

I always assumed one was more of an attainable goal than the other.

"If you think being a big-time NFL player is going to get you out of carrying equipment out to the field, you're very mistaken, my friend."

I turned to face Isa, and my breath hitched in my chest.

I wished I'd had a warning, because seeing her standing mere inches away from me in a black crop-top T-shirt, paired with a matching backward baseball cap, all but did me in. Isa looked gorgeous all done up this morning, but seeing her like this sent a wave of nostalgia through me I couldn't shake.

I gulped, hard, hoping she didn't notice how thrown off-kilter I was by her presence. I forced myself to look away from her long, toned legs. They seemed to go on forever. My focus shifted to the way her tight cutoff jean shorts hugged her hips.

Did she have these same curves before?

Maybe I just pushed the idea of them to the back of my mind.

After all, there was nothing forgettable about her body.

"Never," I managed to get out.

"Also," she grinned mischievously as we walked to the storage closet on the far end of the field, "I brought a couple of boards if you wanted to hang out after this."

"Boards, as in *skate*boards?"

One of the first things I bought with my paper route money

was a skateboard. I was so desperate to find something—anything —in which to bond with Isa. I fell on my ass a lot when I first started. Once I got it though, I understood why she loved it so much.

I didn't tell her that one of the first things I bought with my signing bonus was a custom board. I didn't admit that my favorite way to spend a Saturday morning in Miami was skating down to the beach.

Or that, one night, when I looked through her Instagram, I found a video of her skateboarding downtown with some of her friends. It was my favorite thing to watch when I was homesick— both for Fox Hollow and *her*.

"No, surfboards," she deadpanned. "Yes, skateboards. Unless you're afraid to get hurt?"

Terrified, Bug.

Admittedly though, my fear had nothing to do with getting on a skateboard.

"Me? Afraid?" I scoffed. "I thought we covered this last night. I'm not scared of anything, remember?"

She pulled a single silver key from the pocket of her shorts. "All right, superstar. Grab the blocking sleds."

ISA

THE EQUIPMENT SHED was actually more like a small equipment *building*.

It was filled with new or almost-new equipment, most of it purchased personally by my father himself.

We always lived modestly, in spite of my dad's former profession. My childhood home had three bedrooms. Dad's truck was ten years old. Mom loved shopping at discount stores like Marshall's and TJ Maxx. Their idea of a good time was rummaging through flea markets for hidden treasures and strolling through the farmers' market downtown on a Saturday morning.

None of his kids—whether it was me and Javier or the boys he coached—had ever gone without, though. My father never asked for anything from anyone unless it was for the team. Every year he hosted two charity events, and all proceeds went to Fox Hollow's athletic department.

The whole region came to our town on Sundays to watch the Bluecoats play. The Bluecoats represented Massachusetts. No one in this state loved them more than we did in Fox Hollow, but they weren't just *ours*. We had to share the team.

The Fox Hollow High School team, however, was ours and ours alone.

Businesses closed early on Friday nights. Teachers never gave homework that day. It wasn't just the high school's team, it was the whole town's.

"Need a hand?" a gruff voice behind me asked, causing me to drop the mesh bag full of footballs to the ground.

Seething anger filled me when I found myself face-to-face with Devon McDaniels.

Like Jake, he was wearing black athletic shorts and a heather gray T-shirt with navy-blue lettering. While Jake's shirt said "Fox Hollow Football Alumni," Devon's read "Fox Hollow Football Staff."

I had forgotten that earlier this summer, my dad asked if I'd be upset if he hired Devon as the team's offensive line coordinator. At the time, it took everything in me not to burst out laughing. It was incredibly thoughtful and so like my dad to be concerned about me first.

As far as me caring about Devon, though? Anything I felt for him was ancient history.

At least, until I found out he went around telling people he slept with me, *after* I broke up with him.

"Isa, hi. I came out to the field as soon as your dad said you were here." He grinned. "It'll be like old times."

"Are we talking about before or after you lied about having sex with her?"

I let out a breath as I heard Jake's voice behind Devon. There was no way this was going to end well.

Jake's tone *seemed* level, almost emotionless. But I'd seen the dangerous look in his eyes too many times before a game. It only took one hit, or for the wrong person to say the wrong thing, for him to snap. Jake wasn't a violent person by nature, but when he lost that composure, he'd become a person I didn't recognize.

"I'll grab the rest, Bug," Jake said to me, as he grabbed one of the footballs that had tumbled out of the bag I dropped. He lowered his voice before adding, "I'll behave. I promise."

JAKE

I forgot Devon the Lying Piece of Shit McDaniels worked for Coach Coleman.

As soon as I saw him beelining toward the equipment shed, I dropped everything in my hands. There wasn't enough time to even process what I was doing before I was eavesdropping outside of the door.

Sure, I guessed people could change. The smug smirk on his face told me everything I needed to know, though. I saw it all the time with guys in the league. Men who threw an abundance of charm at women in the hopes that their good looks and status would be enough of a distraction. Those guys were looking for one thing. I knew. I *was* that guy before.

Truth be told, if I weren't back home, I probably still would be.

Models. Actresses. Cheerleaders. Socialites. None of them ever came to my condo. It was always their house or a hotel. And it never happened twice. It didn't matter how good the sex was— always a one and done.

"Well, if it isn't Jake Pierce, stepping down from his throne to mingle with the common folk." Devon's condescending sent a jolt of adrenaline through my veins. "What did we ever do to deserve this honor?"

I will not punch him.
I will not punch him.

I will not punch him.

"I'm here because my mentor asked me to come and show the boys what a *real* football player looks like." I knew taking that jab at him would make him angry.

Due to a patellar tear during our sophomore year of high school, Devon was forced to hang up his cleats. After college, he ended up coming back to Fox Hollow to ask Coach Coleman for a job.

"Did you bring someone?" he shot back.

Before I could answer him, Coach Coleman's voice boomed from behind me. "If you two are done comparing dick sizes, could you please join us on the field? Players are starting to show up."

I fought back a laugh before I apologized and followed him out to the field.

It didn't matter what I did for a job, how much money I had in the bank, or who I was; when Coach spoke, I listened. So, I decided in that moment that I would just steer clear of Devon for the remainder of the practice.

Some things—some people—just weren't worth it.

At that, the sound of Isa's laughter caught my attention.

But, so did the arms wrapped around her.

ISA

"JAKE DIDN'T SAY anything about you coming! The boys are going to be so excited. You guys and Jake?! Hell, I'm excited," I said.

Fox and Lynx Mendez both beamed at my reaction.

Reel it in, Isa.

You would think I'd never been around professional football players before.

Or that I hadn't *just* seen the Mendez twins last night.

"Fellas," Jake exclaimed as he joined us.

They took turns pulling each other into a bro-hug. You know the one. It started with a handshake that turned into a half hug, finalized by loud, hearty claps on the back.

Jake's voice dropped when he continued with, "What are you guys doing here?"

"I called the gym to see if you were still there. I was told you'd be here. I hope it's okay that we crashed." The hesitation in Fox's voice surprised me. This man was a future Hall of Fame quarterback. He'd broken countless records. The Bluecoats had gone to the Super Bowl four times under his helm. Yet, here he was making sure Jake was okay with him being here. "We can dip out if it's not."

Jake scoffed at him. "Are you kidding me? Isa's right. The boys are going to be so excited. Hell, I am too." He winked at me before he turned his attention back to Fox and Lynx. "Wanna throw a bit while we wait? See how long it takes everyone to notice you're here?"

Laughing, the Mendez brothers headed out to the middle of the field.

Without another word, Jake grabbed a football and began to jog out to the field. About halfway to the fifty-yard line, he stopped and turned back. The corners of my own lips tilted up at the sight of his growing smile.

"Hey, Bug," he called out. "If the offer to board after this is still on the table, I'm in."

I wasn't naïve; that was conveyed with intent. I didn't know what was said in the equipment shed, but both Devon and Jake came out with their heads hung after my father went to get them.

Devon stood just a few feet away from me now, with other members of the coaching staff. Jake was making it known, loud and clear, that we were going to hang out. And, I would be sure to call him out on it later while we were skateboarding.

"Go play football, superstar." I grinned, holding up my camera. "I have a job to do."

For the next ten minutes, I focused on Jake, Fox, and Lynx, as they ran drills with the handful of players that were warming up on the field. As more players started to show up, I caught their reactions when they realized exactly *who* was at their first practice.

Once the initial shock wore off, Dad blew his whistle three times and called everyone in. After introducing Jake, Fox, and Lynx, he introduced me.

"This is Isa Coleman," my dad said proudly. "She's been the team's official photographer since Jake was on the team."

"And, yes, she's pretty." Devon stepped forward as he took it upon himself to add to my dad's speech. "But Isa is Coach's daughter and gets our full respect, do you all understand?"

I didn't know whether I should be mortified or angry that Devon seemed to only correlate respect shown to me when it came to relation with my father.

"Well, now that you've made Isa and everyone else feel uncomfortable," Jake said, laughing awkwardly, "let's play ball, huh?"

Before the two of them could continue their pissing contest at my expense, my dad blew his whistle again. "All right. You know where to go."

Everyone dispersed into their respective groups.

As the coaches called out drills, I made my way around the field for the duration of practice, never staying in one place too long. My camera was focused on Jake helping a young player scramble for the ball, when my dad's voice next to me caused me to jump and lose the moment.

"I'm glad you're here, princess." He smiled knowingly. "Your mother seems to think it has something to do with Jake."

I sighed. *Not him, too.* I could usually count on my dad when it came to this kind of stuff.

"Now, before you get all huffy," he continued, "I'm not here to dig. You know as long as you're happy, I'm happy. I just want you to know that if Jake is the one to make you hap—"

"Dad, I love you. I love Mom. But Jake and I *just* saw each other for the first time after not speaking for six years. Only yesterday. I'm going to need some more time before you guys set a wedding date, okay?"

His eyes widened as he chewed on his lip. "I, uh, I think I need to go coach someone."

Confused, I looked around the field for Jake as Dad sprinted across the field.

"So, we're getting married? Is that what I heard?"

I had been giving my father my complete attention. I didn't realize that, at some point, Jake had come over near the bleachers to get water.

I groaned. "How much did you hear?"

"Just that you needed more time before your parents set our wedding date," he said with a grin. "If my say matters, April through July works best with my football schedule."

I rolled my eyes as he put the water bottle to his lips. When he was mid-sip, I tipped the bottle up. Water poured all over him.

I thought about apologizing for a solid two seconds—until he pulled his soaked shirt up and over his head.

"All right, all right. You got me, but I think it's time we start keeping score again." Jake smirked, tossing his shirt on the bleacher behind us. "Isa: one. Jake: zero."

I should be processing what he was saying.

As teens, we tried to playfully one-up each other all the time. We said we were keeping score, but the truth was...neither of us knew what game we were *actually* playing here. Right now, all I could do was gawk at his stomach. Each one of his abs glistened in the warmth of the sunlight, demanding my undivided attention.

Until I saw the V-dip, of course. I didn't even know what it was actually called. Salem called them "sex lines." I knew some girls referred to them as "V-lines." All I knew right then was that Jake had it—and I'd been staring at it for too long.

"Um...I think it's more like Isa: one. Jake: zero. Jake's abs:

eight." I knew there wasn't any way to hide the fact that I had been ogling him.

A small laugh left his lips. He studied me silently for what felt like forever. I wished he would say something. *Anything*. But just as he opened his mouth, the sound of my dad's whistle calling practice for the night grabbed our attention.

As we walked together to join the others, Jake leaned in. "Stay close to me. I don't want Devon thinking he gets to talk to you."

JAKE

AFTER PRACTICE, Isa handed her camera bag to her dad with hesitation.

"Please take it right into the house," she told him. "I'm trusting you, Daddy."

"I will protect it with my life." He chuckled. His smile disappeared when he saw Isa wasn't laughing. "I promise I won't let anything happen to your baby."

I had to bite the corner of my cheek to stop myself from snickering when he opened the passenger door of his truck and proceeded to buckle the camera bag into the seat.

I didn't remember Coach being this fresh when we were growing up, but he was on top of his shit today.

"Before you two head out, I want a picture," he insisted as he pulled his cell phone out of his shorts pocket. "It makes me happy to see you kids back together again."

Isa didn't skip a beat before telling him he was growing soft in his old age, but she obliged anyway. Wrapping her free arm around my shirtless waist, she smiled on cue as I placed my arm around her shoulder.

Then, there was me, over there like: *you and me both, Coach.*

"Is it okay if I post this on Instaface?" he asked, combining two social media names obliviously and turning his phone to show us the photograph.

"I'm okay with it," I began, turning to Isa. "But there's a good chance people will assume we're together, and I don't know if you want to deal with all that."

A small laugh left her lips. "No one is going to assume you're with *me*, Jake."

Coach looked back and forth between us, waiting for a definitive answer.

"Go ahead, Coach," I answered, before the three of us said our goodbyes.

Once Coach was in his truck, I lowered the skateboard Isa had given me a few minutes ago. "You ready, Bug?"

"Are *you* ready?" she countered.

"I was born ready, babe." I grinned.

The words didn't sound foreign as they left my lips, but as soon as I realized I'd called her *"babe,"* I went into panic mode.

"Isa!" Devon McDaniels called her name from the field, saving me from having to explain why I just dropped a pet name so casually in conversation.

"Go! Go! Go!" Isa urged quickly, before skating out of the parking lot.

A trail of laughter followed her as she made her hasty exit. I put one foot on the deck and gained momentum before hopping on with both feet. So much of street boarding was about feeling— moving *with* your board.

It didn't take long for me to catch up to her. When I did, the sheer joy on her face caused my stomach to tighten. I wished I could capture this moment and keep it forever.

This was the Isa I remembered.

Not the quiet woman who fumbled with her cuticles because my presence made her nervous. She was carefree. I didn't need anything else. Her happiness was enough.

It had to be close to eight o'clock. The setting sun and the pink skies provided the prettiest backdrop as we made our way to downtown Fox Hollow. I'd been back in town for months and I had yet to make my way to Main Street.

For the most part, despite the famous football ties to this town, it was quiet here. Main Street was full of small shops and independently owned restaurants. There were a couple of dance studios and an old arcade that, from the looks of it, still seemed to be the place to hang out on a summer night if you were a teenager.

Stopping at an intersection, Isa smiled. "Looks like we made a clean getaway."

"Leave Devon to me," I told her. "I'll deal with him."

"Don't you dare." The warning in Isa's voice caught me off guard. "I can see the steam coming from your ears, Jake. Leave it alone. If there's anything that needs to be handled, I got it."

I shrugged. "You're the boss, Bug."

"How about we follow through with the tradition of frozen yogurt after practice instead?" she offered, pointing to the small ice cream stand just a few feet away from us.

I shouldn't. I should go home. My alarm was set for five tomorrow. I had my work cut out with training camp. Plus, I was on a self-imposed football season diet. A diet I had already broken during brunch at Salem's.

I was about to say no and explain why, when Isa's lips protruded and formed the most pitiful little pout.

How the hell was I supposed to say no to that?

"Okay, but just one scoop."

ISA

IT WAS WELL past midnight by the time I got home last night.

Despite my attempted assurance I would be fine, Jake refused to go to sleep until he got a text from me saying I'd made it home. Which turned into us texting until closer to one until he stopped answering me.

There was an *"I'm sorry...I fell asleep"* text waiting for me when my six o'clock alarm pulled me from my slumber. Immediate guilt filled me as I replied with an apology of my own.

I was exhausted. I could grab a coffee and be fine, though. Jake, on the other hand, would be running drills in full pads in close to ninety degrees in just a few hours.

Sleepily, I started gathering my clothes for the day. After spending some of the night in the field and then boarding downtown Fox Hollow with Jake, I showered. It made everything easier this morning, with the exception of doing my hair.

Luckily for me, my brother, Adam, and I planned on meeting at my parents' house before training camp. If I left soon, there would be time for my mom to braid my hair before we had to leave for the stadium. Since she'd woken up at five in the morning for as long as I could remember, I didn't hesitate to call her this early.

"Of course, mija," she agreed after I asked her if she'd do me the favor. "Did your brother give you your jersey?"

Yesterday, while I was at football practice, Adam and Javier took a trip to the official Pro Shop outside of the stadium and bought us all number eighty jerseys to wear today.

"He did." I smiled, looking down at it on my bed. "Jake's going to love it."

"I thought so too." She chuckled. "And, he's going to love your surprise. I can't believe you pulled it off so quickly."

After saying bye to my mom, I snapped a photo of the back of the jersey spread across my bed, attaching it to a text.

Me: Today will be the first time I wear a jersey that doesn't have my last name on it. I don't think I've told you how proud of you I am.

I sent it to Jake.

His reply, just moments later, made my heart swell.

Jake: I've never been so excited to see someone wear my jersey.

I didn't tell him who else would be showing up in his jersey today. I pulled mine over my head and stood in front of the full-length mirror.

Not to toot my own horn, but *danggggg* did that "PIERCE" look good on my back.

I almost posted the photo to my Instagram but stopped myself, not knowing exactly where Jake and I stood.

We're friends, I think. Maybe?! I didn't even know.

There was still so much we had to talk about. Things had been so easy—too easy—since Retro. I didn't want to bring up the fact we still hadn't had the "you broke my heart" conversation. Even though I knew it needed to happen.

I was content being in denial. Jake was back in my life. It was what I wanted since the second he left for college. But, I knew I couldn't continue ignoring our past if I wanted him to *stay* in my life.

It could surely wait a day or two, though...

There was too much going on right now to plunge down into the emotional depths of our history.

Like making sure I pulled off the surprise of all surprises.

JAKE

Despite only getting four hours of sleep, I felt like I was ready to take on the world.

Not only would today mark the unofficial start of the football season, but Isa and the rest of the Coleman family would also be in the crowd.

Then, later that night, Isa and I had dinner plans.

I knew I was pushing my luck when it came to her, but I didn't care. If she was willing to give me her time, I'd take it. We had years to make up for.

After sitting in bumper-to-bumper traffic for twenty minutes, I pulled into the stadium's VIP parking lot. As soon as I stepped down from my truck, I heard my last name being yelled by multiple people. Only players and people with guest passes were permitted in this lot, so I knew it was safe to turn around and greet whoever it was behind me.

I wasn't ready for the burst of overwhelming emotion that filled me when I saw Coach Coleman, Alma, Abuela, Javier, Adam, Isa...and *my mother* walking toward me. Each of them had on my jersey. Swallowing, I opened my mouth to greet them, but words failed me.

"I told you he would be surprised!" Alma Coleman squealed, grabbing Isa's arms excitedly.

I didn't think twice when Alma called me yesterday to ask if there was any way I could spare an additional VIP pass for a friend of the family that was in town for the weekend.

I never thought that "*friend of the family*" might be my mom.

"When? What? How?" I asked, still incapable of forming complete sentences.

When she reached me, my mom beamed at me and opened her arms. "Hi, baby. Surprise!" Pulling back, with the ear-to-ear smile still on her lips, she said, "It was all Isa. She called me yesterday and set the whole thing up. All I did was pack a bag and show up at the airport."

"*You* did this?" I asked, turning my attention to Isa.

Water pooled in my eyes. I was so overwhelmed by the surprise of seeing my mom here, I hadn't even gotten to take in the sight of Isabel Coleman wearing my jersey. Pride swelled inside of me, knowing it was *my* last name on her back—and especially knowing that, before now, she'd only worn the number eleven Coleman jersey that once belonged to her father.

"Well, it was Javier's idea to wear matching jerseys," she offered, shrugging.

It was so blasé. Like it was no big deal she'd arranged for my mother to come up from Miami in less than twenty-four hours to be here today.

Which was why I didn't even care about the reporters watching us from behind the media line when I closed the space between us...and left her with the feel of my lips on hers.

ISA

THERE WASN'T time to process what happened before Jake pulled away.

As he broke the kiss, he said something about "*talking later*" before he jogged off toward the players' entrance.

Putting my fingers up to my mouth, I desperately searched for something to prove I didn't just imagine his hands cupping my face and pulling me to him. The spearmint lingering on my lips was enough.

"Jake!" I called out. "*Jacob!*"

He stopped in his tracks. The little knots in my stomach tightened, my heart racing as he turned. With shaky legs, I walked to where he stood.

"*Yessss?*" he said, smirking.

Just like that, I felt eighteen again. It didn't matter where we were or who was watching. I was just a girl who'd been kissed by the boy she'd been in love with since their freshman year of high school.

Everything changed in that moment.

Everything was about to change again.

I'd spent the majority of the last couple of days obsessing over the fact that *six years* had passed between us. But maybe Jake and I just weren't ready for something like this at eighteen. Whatever *this* was.

All I knew was I wouldn't run from it this time. Jake Pierce was my first love. I don't think I ever *stopped* loving him. Not really, anyway. There were some things—some people—that never left you all the way.

"You shouldn't have done that." My voice and legs both shook as I tried to ignore the hordes of photographers calling out to us from behind the media line.

His shoulder slumped as he sighed. "I know. It's just—"

Cutting him off, I grabbed a fistful of his T-shirt in my hand and pulled him closer to me. His dark brown eyes bore into mine and I could have sworn, right then, he saw right down to my soul.

"We have so much to figure out." I swallowed when he nodded. My voice was barely above a whisper. "But I'm not running from you—from this—anymore."

"Good."

His one hand gripped my waist while the other cupped my face, his fingertips pushing into the back of my neck while the pad of his thumb caressed my cheek. Every move was deliberate, calculated. And, this time, I soaked it all in.

I was hyper-aware of everything around us. The reporters were calling Jake's name, desperate to pull his attention and get the scoop.

Our mothers squealed behind us as I pressed up on my toes and closed the space between us. As soon as our lips touched again, I allowed my body to mold against his. Suddenly it didn't matter about the time that had passed. It didn't matter who was watching or what else anyone else thought. All that mattered was me and Jake.

I'd always heard about kisses that felt like fireworks. Until now, I thought it was romanticized bullshit. But every passing moment felt *more* than the last. More intense. More real. Just, *more.*

Within seconds, I was addicted to the taste of him. Greedily, I gripped harder. I kissed faster. And when I felt his cock harden against me, a whimpered moan escaped my lips.

Okay. We needed to stop before I followed him into the locker room.

Deep, masculine cheering next to us helped bring us back down to reality.

"Yeahhh, Pierce!"

"Get it, Isa!"

Fox and Lynx walked past us, and Jake and I both burst out laughing.

"I really gotta go, Bug." He grinned, sneaking in one last kiss before pulling away. "I'll see you out there."

JAKE

Once word got around the locker room about Isa and our parking lot kiss, the guys were all over me. Half of them wanted to know who she was. The other half just wanted to give me a hard time.

Any other given day, being razzed by the team would have fired me up. I would have shot back some dickish remark, but not today. They could say whatever they wanted—as long as it wasn't disrespectful to Isa.

And they weren't. Not after they found out she was Roger Coleman's daughter.

Coach Coleman was idolized in this locker room. To me, he

was just "Coach"—Isa and Javi's dad. The reality, however, was that he was one of the greatest quarterbacks to ever play football, and he was also a class act. Everyone who was part of the Bluecoats organization respected him not only as a player—and now a coach —but as a man.

Especially because he did things he didn't have to, like spending a week in Montana with the new generation of players, or taking Fox out to dinner to celebrate the records he broke that Coach himself had made when *he* was a player. The fact that he retired from playing just to coach the football players of the future was admirable from a player standpoint as well.

"You're brave, man." Ty Ashland laughed as he grabbed his helmet from the locker next to mine. "I don't know if I would have the balls to go after Roger Coleman's daughter."

No one in this room knew Coach the way I did.

It was never about *"having the balls"* as Ty so eloquently put it. It was about having respect for a man who took me into his home, treated me like his own son, and taught me everything he knew about the game. He trusted me. I never wanted to betray that.

We never talked about Isa or what happened between me and her.

"You know, you can ask about her." Coach had laughed as we sipped on bourbon on the front porch steps. "Isa. We can talk about her."

"I've wanted to," I admitted. "But I knew, given what happened between us, I was just lucky you and Mama A still wanted me to be part of your lives. I wasn't about to jinx that."

"You know, for a long time, Alma and I were pretty convinced you two would end up together." He chuckled. "And...I'm honestly not sure what happened between you two. Isa never talked about it either. All I know is that I haven't heard that laugh—the one only you seem to be able to pull from her—since you left for Alabama."

So, I told him. Everything. At least, my side of things. I even confessed that part of the reason I didn't make a move on her in high school was because I didn't want to disrespect him.

He didn't say much. He had sat there quietly, listening as I rambled on about how I fell in love with his only daughter.

Before we called it a night, he shook my hand.

"For the record, son, I would've been okay with it. And, if the day ever comes again, I still would be."

His words played back in my head now as I pulled my practice jersey on over my head. That conversation had taken place just a few months ago. I hoped he meant what he'd said.

"All right, Casanova," Fox's voice behind me grabbed my attention, "you ready to make the rest of New England fall in love with you too?"

For the first time in my life, I was—ready. For football...and maybe love, too.

"Let's do this."

ISA

A SMALL WAVE of relief washed over me when Jake led me out to the backyard.

A person could change a lot in six years.

I wasn't saying that a secret sex room would be a deal-breaker, but it would have been a bit more to take in than the picnic currently set out on the lawn.

After training camp, Jake and I had gone our separate ways for the remainder of the afternoon. He had lunch with his mom—who was staying in my parents' guest room—and I worked on editing the photos from last night's practice.

Or...I *tried* to edit.

To say I was distracted would be an understatement. While I should have been working on contrast and focus, all I could think about was getting to Jake's.

And kissing him again.

The amount of restraint it took not to pounce on him the second he opened the door was actually quite embarrassing.

"Jacob Pierce!" I squealed now, clutching his arm. "You have a telescope?!"

His laughter as I practically skipped over to the tripod set up next to the blanket made my heart swell.

"So, I know it's too early still," he started when he joined me, "but the Isa I remember used to get so excited over the moon. And I'm sure you already know this, but there's a full moon tonight. I guess I thought the chance to check it out might keep you here longer."

When I was a little girl, I wanted to be an astronaut. There was nowhere I wanted to go more than the moon. I was obsessed. As I grew, my career goals changed, but never my love for the lunar object that orbited our earth.

Most people spent time chasing sunrises or basking in sunsets. My favorite part of the day had always been when I realized the moon was hanging in the sky. I looked for it each night.

And, Jake remembered.

"You know," I began, sighing dreamily as I looked up to the sky, "legend has it that the sun and moon were lovers forced to chase each other back and forth across the sky."

"Sounds like a couple of kids I once knew." Kicking his slide-on sandals off onto the lawn next to the red plaid blanket laid out on the grass, he sat down.

I pulled my Chucks off and then cursed under my breath as I attempted to push my socks off with my heels like I'd done with my shoes.

My plan backfired when I lost my balance. I tried to steady myself as I stumbled back, but before I knew it, I fell flat on my ass.

"And suddenly, it makes sense why your dad would randomly call you 'Grace.'" Jake chuckled as he connected a small Bluetooth speaker to his phone. "How 'bout some music?"

"Yeah, Jake. I'm fine, thanks." I rolled my eyes and then glared in his direction.

"I've seen you fall enough times in our lives to know when you're okay and when you're not," he mused, laughing and extending his hand as he leaned over to me.

"But I'm oooold now," I whined. I waved him off as I stood up from the grass. "I could break a hip or something."

"You're twenty-four, Isa." He reached over the cooler placed on the edge of the blanket and popped the cover off. "I figured we'd kick it old school. I made peanut butter and strawberry preserve sandwiches. There are purple grapes and carrot chips and roasted red pepper hummus too. Oh! And, blueberry iced tea from Sunnycrest."

"Okay, how'd you pull this off?" I questioned, noting he'd collectively made a meal of my favorite snacks. Some of the things are the same—like my love for purple grapes *specifically*—but carrot chips and hummus and Sunnycrest Farm's blueberry iced tea were new favorites of mine.

"I may have had some help." At the sight of my wide eyes, he let out a small laugh. "I asked your mom."

"You asked my mom?!" I groaned. "Jacob Pierce, you know better than that! She's going to want to know e-v-e-r-y-thing that happens tonight."

Mom, Abuela, and Ruth Pierce spent the majority of training camp talking about how excited they were that Jake and I were finally "*an item*." Despite me telling them— repeatedly—that I wasn't sure where Jake and I stood, none of them seemed to hear it.

"Yeah." He grinned. "If it makes you feel any better, I got to spend the entire lunch answering *my* mom's questions. I swear that woman worked for the FBI in a past life."

"Can we please talk about the music?" I asked, changing the subject. Deflecting in uncomfortable situations was my specialty. "Did you find some magical playlist that happens to have all my favorite songs? I'm going to need that link."

"Or...I made one?" He shrugged, handing me his phone.

I swallowed when I saw "Isa's Mix" at the top of the playlist. My fingers swept through a list of over thirty songs from blink-182, Simple Plan, Sum 41, Good Charlotte, Fall Out Boy, and every other pop-punk band that had stolen my heart as a teenager.

"I can send it to you, though," he offered.

"That's adorable." The sarcasm laced in my voice was a little heavier than intended. "How many other girls have you done this for, Romeo?"

"Try zero," he shot back defensively. "Gym, training, home, sleep—that's my life. Oh, and on Sundays during the off-season, I golf."

I chuckled. "And with my dad of all people. You know, when he said he was golfing with some '*buddies*,' I was picturing old dudes—well, around my dad's age—not you and the Mendez brothers."

Lynx's comment about having the utmost respect for my father when we first met suddenly made a lot more sense. I assumed it was just because he knew my dad as Roger Coleman: Hall of Fame quarterback. Not because he knew the ugly sweater vests and khaki shorts version of my dad.

"You know, it's kind of cute you've been stalking me on Instagram," he said, taking a sip of his iced tea before he continued. "Fox and Lynx only came the one time, and I'm the only one that posted about it."

"It's kind of cute you think I was stalking you, and not Fox or Lynx. I'm sure you tagged them. It probably just showed up in their tagged photos." My response was bullshit, and Jake's narrowed eyes and smirk told me he knew it, too. Of course it was Jake I'd been creeping on.

"And to think I was going to ask you to be my date to the ring ceremony with me on Sunday," he hinted, shaking his head. "I can see if Fox and Lynx are available, though. If ya want."

Holy shit.

The ring he was talking about was a *Super Bowl* ring.

You know, because he played and won the Super Bowl last February.

Just the biggest sporting event in the entire world. *No big deal.*

"Do you think the music will be as good there as it is here at Château de Pierce?" I asked, pretending like I wasn't internally freaking the fuck out.

He chuckled at my response. "Nah, but I heard Snoop Dogg might be there. Diddy was at the last ring ceremony."

"All right, I'm in," I agreed, as nonchalantly as possible. I tried to keep that same level of cool as I said, "So, if people ask who I am to you, what do you want me to say?"

"It would probably be easier to just say you're my girlfriend," he suggested.

"Are you sure that's a good idea? The media is already having a field day with our kiss," I noted. "I don't know if I'm fake-girl-friend material." I'd seen the Hallmark movies. I knew how that always panned out.

"No one ever said anything about you being my *fake* girlfriend, Bug."

The emphasis he put on the word "*fake*" made me pause for a moment.

"Before you shut it down, hear me out," he started. "As much as it hurt, I never stopped loving you. If you tell me you don't want this too, I'll never push again. But, I know what I want. It's the same thing I've always wanted. The question is, do you want it too?"

JAKE

I DIDN'T KNOW who I thought I was pretending to be, walking into Retro thinking I could just pretend that my life had been fine without Isa. That man didn't exist. He never existed. If he did, I would be able to stop my emotions from spilling out of my mouth every time she was around.

I wished I could make sense of it all. Everything between us was moving at lightning speed—mostly because of my own doing. But, as I just told her, I knew what I wanted.

I wanted her—every part of her. I wanted her heart, her soul. I wanted to be her favorite hello and her hardest goodbye.

There were new dips and curves of her body I was aching to discover.

Mostly, I just wanted to be able to kiss her whenever I felt like it.

If I'd learned anything about my feelings for Isa over the last forty-eight hours, it was that nothing was partial.

It was emotional. It was physical. It was everything, all at once.

And, it always had been.

When things weren't okay, it went beyond sadness. It was all-consuming. The idea of living a life without her had made me sick to my stomach. I didn't eat. I was skipping gym sessions. If I hadn't gotten away from Fox Hollow, who knew how long I would have lived like that.

This time, I knew the risk.

I also knew I would regret it for the rest of my life if I didn't take another chance.

Despite my effort to seem neutral when I asked her what she wanted, I knew I wasn't subtle in my approach. And even though I took a bite of watermelon a few moments before dropping the "*girlfriend*" bomb on her, I was parched. There was no way she couldn't see how off-balance I was.

I've had three-hundred-pound men run straight at me to pull me down, and that sounded like a fucking walk in the park right now compared to the anxiety brewing inside my chest.

The pressure I put on her was a lot; I knew that. But her silence was killing me slowly.

"Isa, please," I begged. "Say something. Anything."

The juice from the watermelon slice I was holding dripped down my hand. It didn't matter, though. I simply watched her lips as I waited for her answer. There was a primal instinct kicking in I had never felt before. Like a lion waiting to pounce at the perfect moment.

Looking me in the eyes, she finally said, "You. Us. I want all of it."

ISA

Nature was so loud, from the constant chirping of cicadas to the happy songs of sparrows fluttering in the branches of the pine trees. The wind picked up speed, moving the humid summer air around us.

The sun was nowhere to be found. Off to chase the moon, I supposed.

All the background noise disappeared when Jake pushed everything between us forward in one swooping motion. In just as much time, he pulled me onto his lap. A mousey squeak left my lips as I found myself straddled over him.

Instinctively, I pressed my hands to his chest to steady myself. His own hands had made their way under my rising tank top and onto my lower back.

"Hi."

"Hi, boyfriend."

"So, it's official?" he asked as he pulled me closer to him.

By the time I nodded, there was no space between our bodies.

"Good." He grinned and pressed his forehead to mine. "Because I swore I wouldn't do this until you were mine."

"Do what?" I asked coyly.

"Let me show you." Jake's hands trailed from my back to my sides, over my hips, the outline of my breasts, and up my neck, until they stopped at my face. As he brought my face to his, I closed my eyes.

I expected eager, hungry kisses like the ones we shared in the parking lot earlier. Instead, I got the slow, deep, deliberate kind.

It didn't matter that the clouds above us grew darker with every passing moment. We were still lost in each other when the rain began. Within minutes, the precipitation began to settle in the fabric of my top, my hair hanging heavier as it soaked up the rain. I pulled back, reaching for the food scattered along the blanket.

"Jake!" I giggled when he took the container of the grapes from my hand and placed them back down on the blanket.

"Leave it," he murmured, before pulling my bottom lip into his. "I'll order you a pizza."

"Stop it!" I laughed, pushing my body back until I was off his lap. "Help me bring this stuff inside."

As we quickly threw everything in the cooler, the rolling thunder shook the earth around us.

"You go on in," he said as my eyes widened in fear. "I'll be right there."

For a split second, I debated whether or not I should stay and help him.

But then another loud rumble boomed in the clouds above us.

"Go!" he insisted, grinning knowingly. "I got this, Bug."

There weren't too many things that scared me.

Thunder, though? Thunder terrified me. I wasn't scared of the lightning—you know, the thing that could actually hurt you. Nope, my ass was scared of the big *kaboom*.

Knowing his hands would be full, I waited right inside the sliding door to let him in. By the time he ran up the deck stairs, his shirt was completely soaked. Water droplets fell down his cheeks and covered his arms.

Just as I slid open the door, another clap of thunder exploded in the skies. Jumping back in fear, I let out an inaudible scream.

"Come here, you big baby," he teased, opening his arms as he walked toward me.

"No way! You're soaked." I squealed as he engulfed me in his arms. "Jacob James!"

His laughter echoed in the empty house as I wiggled out of his arms.

"Great." I narrowed my eyes in his direction. "Now I'm all wet too."

He motioned to the hallway. "Well then, let's go get you some dry clothes."

"Jacob Pierce, are you trying to get me naked?"

JAKE

"I'll be on my best behavior."

As I opened my T-shirt drawer, I cursed internally.

I wasn't normally someone to believe in signs, but I was hard-pressed not to believe the thunderstorm hadn't been an intervention of sorts. If the clouds hadn't opened up in a downpour, I would have kept going. It was different with Isa. It *needed* to be more. More than heat-of-the-moment, backyard sex.

We needed to go on a date. A *real* date.

When she opened the door, I groaned. "Damn it."

Almost all self-control flew out the fucking window the second I saw her in my T-shirt. She had pulled together the bottom of the shirt and knotted it in the center.

"Do you have a bag or something I can put my wet shirt in till I get home?" she asked, giving me an opportunity to regain my bearings.

"I'll just toss it in the dryer," I offered, extending my hand for her shirt. "If you want to find a movie or something, I'll meet you in the living room?"

She followed me until I got to the door that led to my basement. Once I got to the washer and dryer, I grabbed the clothes I had forgotten in the dryer yesterday.

I didn't have a housekeeper. For the most part, I even made my own food. Hell, even my house wasn't that big by typical NFL player standards. I didn't need a big house. It was just me.

I didn't understand why single men bought multi-million-dollar homes. *A big empty house all to myself? No thank you.*

Maybe it was because I grew up with Coach Coleman as an example. He could have bought any house he wanted. Fox Hollow may have been a smaller town, but there was a gated community full of those million-dollar homes on the east side. Hugh Fairgrounds lived there. A lot of guys on the team did.

The Colemans lived in the suburban north end of town. Neighborhoods full of backyard pools and white picket fences. It was the perfect place to raise a family. It was exactly what I had in mind when I bought the three-bedroom, split-level ranch style home three houses down from Coach Coleman.

More than anything, I wanted to settle down, have kids, and be the dad I desperately needed growing up. Stefano didn't give me anything—save for the understanding of exactly what I *didn't* want to be. And, beyond that, the understanding of exactly what I *did* want to be as well.

I wanted to chase my dreams. I wanted to make a name for myself. So, later on down the road when I had children of my own, they wouldn't want for anything. They would have me wholeheartedly.

I didn't realize when I bought this house that it'd been in the back of my mind. I wanted a place my children could grow up in that was safe. This street gave me so much security as a child. I longed to give to someone else what the Coleman family had given to me.

Marriage and children were nowhere close to being in my immediate future, but if I was being honest, there was only one person I ever saw myself being with for the long haul.

And, in this moment, she was right in front of me.

ISA

SINCE OUR DINNER was ruined by the downpour, I called in a couple of salads while Jake was downstairs.

"Did you pick a movie?"

I hadn't heard him come back up the stairs, so the unsuspecting company in the room startled me. "I did." I tried my hardest to calm my racing heart as he plopped down on the gray microfiber couch next to me. "I also ordered grilled chicken salads from Fox Hollow House of Pizza. Extra ranch for me. Light Italian for you. I hope I remembered right."

A growing grin spread across his face. "You did. I wondered if you had caved on the whole vegan thing."

Shortly after our senior year of high school began, I decided I wanted to eat a strictly plant-based diet. If it didn't come from the earth, I wasn't putting it in my mouth. My family teased me relentlessly, but there was never a version of dinner I couldn't eat during those two years. Even if it meant Abuela was making me my own meal.

"I commend anyone that commits to being vegan. I just missed cheese." I shrugged. "It was a downward slope back to bacon cheeseburgers after that."

He chuckled. "Also, I appreciate you ordering a salad for yourself. I wouldn't have been mad if you got your jalapeño poppers, though. Can I get you something to drink? I'm pretty sure I have everything needed for palomas."

The tequila-based drink was my mom and abuela's favorite.

We always had tequila, limes, and Fresca in the house growing up. That's why it was my choice of beverage to sneak when I was seventeen.

"So, I actually don't drink anymore." I knew this would come up eventually. Though, it didn't make the moment any less awkward. "But I'll take a water if you have any."

"One water comin' up."

He grinned before he jumped off the couch.

Huh. That was easy. Too easy.

The only thing that separated Jake's kitchen and living room was a small retaining wall.

"What made you decide to give up drinking?" he asked.

I knew it.

However, his question wasn't laced with judgment like most people when I told them I didn't drink alcohol. It was exhausting having to clarify that just because I chose not to have a beer didn't mean I didn't like to have fun.

And, no, I wouldn't take "*just one shot.*"

"I didn't like the person I was becoming when I drank," I admitted. "I was drinking to numb heartbreak...to numb the loss of you."

I paused for a moment when he entered the room again. He didn't say a word when he handed me a glass of ice water. His solemn stance was unreadable, but instead of feeding my fear, I exhaled and continued.

"The first time I had sex—something that'd been so important to me to wait for—I was trashed. It became a cycle. Do something stupid when drinking, drink more to deal with the repercussions the next morning, do something stupid when drinking. I was—"

The doorbell rang, interrupting my explanation. I reached for my clutch, but before I could make it off the couch, Jake was already at the front door.

"Put your wallet away." With his hand on the doorknob, he turned back to face me. "I asked you over for dinner. You're not paying."

When the delivery boy realized he was at Jake Pierce's house, he almost dropped the brown paper bag in his hand. "Holy shit. You're Jake Pierce!"

Jake not only caught the bag before it fell to the ground but proceeded to take the freakout with such grace.

The delivery boy was only sixteen or seventeen. Bright red tufts of curly hair poked out of the little hole of his backward baseball cap.

As soon as Jake saw the heather gray Fox Hollow Football shirt that only players received, he grinned. "You play ball?" Jake asked, scribbling his signature on the napkin the freckle-faced redhead had given him to sign. "What's your name, man?"

"It's, uh, Nick," the delivery boy told him. "And, yeah, I was at practice last night. I'm the backup quarterback, so I got to work with Fox. Coolest moment of my life, man."

"Fox is legit," Jake agreed, obliging when Nick then asked him to take a selfie.

I knew Jake was a big deal now. I saw the way the young players looked up to him last night at practice. Maybe it was because this felt more intimate—more personal—but I was so moved by the moment.

It showed exactly who Jake was as a person.

The world saw him as an up-and-coming football player. He was filled to the brim with talent and potential. Of course, I saw that too. But at the end of the day, he was just Jake to me.

The boy who learned how to skateboard so we had something to do together. He was the one that got a job so he could afford tickets to see *my* favorite band. I knew the selfless, kindhearted man *under* the helmet.

It was why I wasn't questioning the decision I made in the backyard.

Should we have taken more time before deciding to jump right into a relationship? Probably. Waiting would have only prolonged the inevitable, though. Whether it worked or not.

I knew this was crazy.

It was impulsive.

And, exactly what I wanted.

"All right," Jake laughed as he finally closed the door, "where were we?"

"You were just about to kiss me."

ISA

MY EYES FLUTTERED open in panic at the sudden sound of Jake's alarm clock.

"Go back to sleep." Jake chuckled. Seconds later, the droning beep ceased. The weight of the bed shifted as he leaned over and pressed his lips to my forehead. "I have to head to camp, but you can stay as long as you want. If you leave, just lock up before you go."

After we both fell asleep on the couch, Jake suggested I just spend the night. The thought of driving the thirty minutes back home while half-asleep gave me anxiety, so I was all too quick to agree.

He made it crystal clear he wanted to wait to have sex until he had taken me out on a proper date. I pouted, eventually getting him to agree that the Super Bowl ring ceremony counted as a date. After he scooped me up and carried me to his bed like a baby, he even offered to go sleep on the couch. I told him he was an idiot and then proceeded to have the best night of sleep while wrapped up in his arms.

He didn't have to tell me twice that I could go back to sleep.

As soon as my head hit the fluffy pillow, I drifted back into the sweetest slumber.

When I woke up, the concept of time was lost on me. The light-blocking shades that covered Jake's bedroom windows gave no indication of how long I slept. Once I reached over for my phone, I was shocked to see it was almost eleven-thirty. I couldn't remember the last time I slept past eight in the morning. Even on the nights I worked at Retro and didn't get to bed until close to three, I *never* stayed in bed this late.

I'd have to ask Jake where he bought this magical bed. Or maybe complete bliss just wore this girl out.

After unlocking my phone, I found three text threads with new messages.

Two from my brother, one from Jake, and the last from my mother.

Jake: Leaving you in my bed was the hardest thing I've ever had to do.

Javi: I take it dinner went well since you didn't come home last night.

Javi: Heads up. Ma called me. She saw your car @ Jake's when she brought Abuela to her doctor's appt.

Mama: Good morning, mija. Coffee before you go home?

Laughing, I sent my mom a text saying I would be there in a bit. Next, I opened my brother's text and let him know I was alive and would be home after having coffee with Mom.

Then, I stared at Jake's text, re-reading his words before sighing happily.

Isa: This bed is so lonely without you. Grabbing my clothes and heading over to have coffee with my mom. By the time you see this, you'll be done...so, I hope you had a good morning at camp. Talk to you later.

Even though we came to the conclusion last night that we were an item—an exclusive item, at that—I wasn't sure what the ground rules were for something like this. Our relationship was new territory, not only for both of us but for me in general. Relationships, exclusivity, all of that was a pretty foreign concept to me.

Sure, I had dated, but nothing ever stuck. The closest thing I had to something solid was with Wes, and the six months we spent together. Our relationship began after we met at a mutual friend's bonfire last fall. Before he left for the night, he asked for my number. Three days later, he asked me to dinner.

Things seemed to be going in the right direction. We talked about the future. He helped me put a portfolio together, introduced me to a few banker friends, and helped me through the process of buying the building that would eventually become my art gallery.

On paper, things were perfect.

But just as the saying went, if it seemed too good to be true, it probably was.

We ended things when he told me he had a problem with how involved my family was in my life.

In a way, I understood. It was a lot. My family could be a lot.

I knew relationships required compromise, but telling me I needed to walk away from my family? That was never going to happen. So, I walked away from Wes instead.

In hindsight, I should have known it wasn't going to work out in the end. We had nothing in common. It went well beyond the whole "opposites attract" thing. His friendships were all based around work. Colleagues, clients, or connections made in the banking industry.

Hell, I didn't know there was an entire inside world of banking before Wes and I started dating.

He didn't understand why I would want to go to Salem's just to hang out. The concept of weekly Sunday dinners at my parents' house was seen as a chore instead of something to look forward to.

We shared nothing meaningful. Nothing had substance. We never just stayed home, content being in each other's company. There was always some sort of event to attend. I tried to pretend I was okay with it, but the relief I felt when we ended things proved otherwise.

We ended things last March. Since then, I had gone on a few first dates. There were no second dates, though. So instead, I focused on my photography. If I wasn't shooting, editing, or developing, I was working in the downtown office space that—once it was gutted, renovated, and painted—would eventually be the home of Coleman Collective. A gallery—*my* gallery—that would feature local photographers and artists, including my own work.

Which reminded me, I had to stop by my parents' house anyway.

My dad still had my camera. I had already spent far too long without it. Even though it'd only been twenty-four hours, it felt like a piece of me was missing.

At the sound of my phone ringing, I sighed. I expected to have to reiterate to my impatient mother that I'd be there in just a few *more* minutes. But at the sight of Jake's name on the screen, an ear-to-ear smile spread across my face.

"Hey, you," I answered.

With my phone in one hand, I clutched my rumbling stomach with the other. Thankfully, I knew Mom and Abuela would both jump to feed me as soon as I mentioned being hungry.

"Hey, I only have a few seconds before I have to go back out for the press conference, but I just wanted to call and say hi."

"Hi." I beamed at the sound of Jake's voice coming through the phone. "How was camp?"

"Good. Crazy. There were so many people here." He chuckled. "So, I know we didn't talk about hanging out tonight or anything, but are you around? I have lunch plans with my mom, and it would have to be low key because I have to get up early again tomorrow, but honestly, I just want to see you again."

"I actually have plans," I started. "But they're low key too and I know you'd be more than welcome."

"Are you sure?" he asked. "I don't want to impose."

"I'm having dinner with Salem. She'd be mad if you didn't come."

JAKE

ONE OF THE perks of being native to Fox Hollow was knowing there were certain places I could go where the owners would make sure I could eat or shop in peace. I tried not to take advantage of my "hometown boy" status too often, but there were always special exceptions to the rule.

My momma being home certainly qualified as one of those.

So, when she asked if we could have lunch at The Village Kitchen—her favorite artisan sandwich shop downtown—I didn't think twice before calling up the owner and name-dropping to secure us a quiet table in the back.

When we arrived, the hostess very discreetly took us to a corner booth.

Had I known Kelsie Madden would be our server, I might have reconsidered the whole thing altogether.

I heard her before I saw her.

"Well, if it isn't my faaaaavorite ex-boyfriend!"

So much for flying under the radar.

Despite the fact that I hadn't seen Kelsie since her party after the Senior Bye-B.Q., she greeted me like we were old friends.

I couldn't remember if I'd even spoken to her at the party. Still feeling the high of Isa's kiss, I had walked in on cloud nine. It didn't last long, though. I crashed down *hard* when Devon, proud as a peacock, bragged on about how he *"fucked Fox Hollow's Virgin Mary."*

It'd been six years, and she ruined any chance of me assuming she wasn't being nice because of my status when she completely ignored my mother's presence upon walking up to the table.

"You know, I heard you were back in town." Kelsie smirked, not breaking eye contact with me as she dropped two drink napkins down onto the table.

"So did every sports news outlet that reported it," my mom muttered under her breath. She made no effort to hide her dramatic eye roll when Kelsie not only ignored her but asked if we could take a picture together.

"For old time's sake."

I started to tell her I didn't think it was appropriate, but she shoved her phone in my mom's hand.

"Okay, sure." I sighed. "But then can we order something to drink?"

She agreed and went back to ignoring my mother as soon as her phone was back in her hand. "What can I get you?"

"I'll have an iced tea, please," my mom answered before looking at me. "You should probably have water. I imagine you and Isa will have lots of champagne on your date tonight. Want to make sure you're hydrated."

"Mother knows best." I shrugged, looking up to Kelsie. The perky excitement from moments ago was gone. Her shoulders were slouched, and a frown had settled on her lips. "Just a water for me, please."

Without a word, Kelsie walked away from the table. As soon as I saw her head back into the kitchen, I burst out into laughter.

"Wow, Mom, you certainly mastered the art of subtlety. Also, I wasn't aware Isa and I were going on a date tonight."

"What?" she asked, feigning innocence. "I must have gotten the days mixed up. The ring ceremony isn't tonight? I mean, I didn't realize I had to be subtle about the fact that you have a girlfriend."

Narrowing my eyes, I shook my head in amusement. "Are you sure that was about Isa? Or was it more because you never liked Kelsie?"

"Why can't it be both?" she asked, as a different server returned with our drinks.

Kelsie was nowhere to be found for the rest of our lunch. Ben, the server that took over, either didn't care about who I was or didn't know. Either way, it was a welcome change.

After the lunch plates were cleared and dessert was ordered, my mom sighed. "You know, I thought I was happy in Florida, but the more time I spend back here in Fox Hollow, the more I start to think that, maybe, it might be time to come back home."

"It's funny, isn't it?" I started. "I didn't realize how much this place meant to me until I was back here."

There was a brief pause in our conversation as Ben dropped down the lemon cake Mom and I chose to share.

"The place, the people..." Mom said as soon as Ben walked away. "I feel like I've just gotten to know Isa. I didn't get the chance to really know her when you two were teenagers, and I don't want to be on the outside of your life."

"You'd never be on the outside of my life," I assured her. "But I certainly wouldn't be sad to have you close by."

After we finished our cake, I settled the bill. Looking down at my phone for the first time since we sat down, I found a text from Isa on my lock screen.

Isa: Turns out you can't even go out to lunch without it making it to Instagram. Be sure to tell Kelsie your girlfriend says hi.

I chuckled as I unlocked it and typed a return text.

Me: Don't worry. My mom had your back.

JAKE

The next few days were a whirlwind.

Between training camp, trying to spend as much time as I could with my mom before she went back to Miami to start packing, and Abuela's birthday party, by the end of Saturday night, I was running on fumes.

It was all worth it, though—especially seeing Abuela's happy tears when she realized everything that had been done specifically for *her,* including her surprise reunion with her sisters. She thanked me a hundred times for being there, as if I would have missed it. Even if Isa and I hadn't been able to find our way back to each other the way we had, I would have made sure to at least stop by. The Colemans were just as much family to me as my own mother.

I certainly wasn't sad about spending the night dancing with Isa and filling my stomach with Mama Alma's food, though.

Two-a-days were set to begin on Tuesday. The first pre-season game of the year was coming up on Thursday. But tonight, we would celebrate.

Instead of driving home at midnight when the party wrapped up last night, Isa came three houses down to mine. Once again, she fell asleep watching a movie. Instead of moving her this time, I covered her up with a blanket and took the other side of the sectional myself.

The warm summer sunlight on my cheeks woke me up. I opened my eyes and expected to see Isa still sound asleep on the couch. Instead, I found the blanket I had covered her up with folded nice and neat over the pillow I had slid under her head.

Disappointment settled in my stomach only to be quickly replaced with relief when I heard coffee percolating in the kitchen. The robust smell of the dark roast quickly wafted over the retainer wall. I kicked off the comforter I pulled from my bed and began to make my way toward the caffeine.

With her back still turned to me, Isa greeted me. "Good morning, sleepyhead. I was going to wake you up as soon as your coffee was done."

"Mornin', yourself." I grinned as I took in the sight of my messy kitchen. I've cooked chicken on the grill out back before, but I was fairly certain this was the first time food had been prepared on the stovetop since I moved in. Even if I could cook. "Whatcha making?"

"Banana protein pancakes." She smiled. "I called my dad and asked him what you could eat. You had everything I needed but the bananas. Luckily, my parents had some, so I just shopped in their kitchen."

That explained the sweatpants and the T-shirt she was wearing. The black joggers didn't look like something she would normally wear.

"I also shopped in the closet of Alma Coleman." She laughed, noticing me taking in her appearance. "The pancakes will be ready in a few minutes, but you can get started on your coffee."

"Where did you come from, Isa Coleman?" I asked, grinning as I walked closer to her.

"Three doors down."

As she shrugged, I pulled her to me by her waist and took a moment to appreciate her beauty.

With a small smile on her face, she pushed me off her gently. "Jake! The pancakes are gonna burn."

Reluctantly, I let her go. I would have been fine with eating the fresh fruit bowl in my fridge, but knowing Isa had gone through the trouble to make something for me, I wasn't about to be the asshole who messed up her plan.

After she returned to the griddle, I took a seat on the bench of the farmer's table up against the wall.

"I hate to be the bearer of bad news, but as soon as I'm done cleaning this mess up, I have to head back over to my mom's. Apparently she doesn't trust my judgment when it comes to making sure I have something appropriate to wear tonight."

Tonight.

I could hardly wait for tonight.

For a multitude of reasons.

Don't get me wrong, I was excited for the ceremony. I was excited to have my Super Bowl ring. But, I was most excited to walk into Hugh Fairgrounds' home with Isa on my arm...and then go home with her afterward.

I imagined tonight was like the male equivalent of losing your virginity on prom night. You know, minus the whole being a virgin thing.

"Jake? You okay?" she asked, handing me a plate with three massive banana pancakes on them. "You've been awfully quiet."

"Just thinking about tonight," I told her honestly.

"Are you *nervous?*" she teased. "I mean, you already won the game..."

"My nerves have nothing to do with football, Bug."

ISA

For the most part, Alma Coleman dressed like your everyday suburban housewife. My mom lived in leggings and athletic wear. So, she'd pull out all the stops for my dad's football events and their date nights.

I had rolled my eyes when she insisted we go shopping together this morning, but secretly, I was thankful for the help. She had been to more of these events before I was born than I'd gone to in my entire life.

In the midst of the chaos of the morning, I forgot Jake's mother was staying in my parents' guest room. When I walked into the kitchen and saw her sitting with my mom, chatting over coffee, I stopped in my tracks.

"Mija!" My mother beamed at the sight of me. "I was just telling Ruth that Jasmine and Franco were so excited to get a call this morning. They'll be here at three to do your hair and makeup."

"Mommmmm." I groaned. "I told you not to go crazy."

"As if I was going to listen," she scoffed. "Abuela should be ready. Why don't you go get her and meet us outside?"

It was of no surprise that there wasn't a single trace of last night's party to be found around the house. All of the decorations had been taken down, the trash removed, and per usual, the counters and floors shined. I wouldn't doubt that my mother had gotten up long before the sun to get her house back in order.

Knocking on the wall outside of Abuela's open door, I poked my head into her room.

"Morning, Abuela. Mom said to tell you we're heading out soon to get a dress for me to wear tonight. I was surprised to hear you were coming, you little dancing queen!"

She chuckled at my reference to her dancing with Jake, Javier, and Adam last night. She spent just as much time with us on the portable dance floor my parents rented for the night as she did sitting down, catching up with her sisters.

When Fox and Lynx Mendez stopped by to drop off some game day tape for Jake, they ended up staying—at Abuela's insistence—and she conveniently kept finding more excuses to stay with us.

Because my parents didn't have enough guest rooms, one already preoccupied with Jake's mom, Abuela's sisters opted to crash at the hotel in town.

"Should we call Tia Rosa and Tia Josefina?" I asked.

The thought of having an audience as I tried on dresses was daunting, but I knew Abuela's time with her sisters was limited.

Abuela waved me off, though. She said they were taking the morning to rest after all the chaos of traveling and then the party. She grabbed her purse from her nightstand, and then we met Ruth and my mom outside to make our way to the mall.

After three stores, just as many hours, and no dress in hand, I started to lose hope.

I sighed as I reached for the last dress hanging on the dressing room door. I knew it as soon as I stepped into the dress: this was the one.

I never would have chosen the yellow chiffon maxi dress for myself. Blue roses were scattered on the fabric, making it look more like a piece of art than an evening gown. The behind-the-neck halter tie, ruffled accents, and a draping flowy skirt brought it all together.

The three gasps that followed once I opened the dressing room door solidified my thoughts.

My mom nodded in approval as I did a spin. "Si, mija. That's la única."

Ruth reached for the tissue box sitting on the glass table between the dressing room sofas. Dabbing her eyes, she began to apologize. "I'm sorry." She let out a small laugh. "I just never got to do stuff like this with Jake. Of course, I love him and I wouldn't have traded the cleats and smelly uniforms for any amount of dance shoes or tutus, but, this was nice. Getting to do this with all of you gave me a small glimpse of what it would have been like to have a daughter. So, thank you."

She turned to me specifically before she continued. "You look beautiful, Isa. For what it's worth, I agree with your mom. That's the dress."

Growing up, I didn't get to see much of Ruth. She was a single mom, and Jake's family wasn't like mine. From what I was told and what I saw later on, they didn't help much. She did it all on her own. Understandably, Jake always spoke so highly of her. To the point that her very presence intimidated me.

She always carried herself with such confidence. Much like my own mother, she didn't look like she was in her fifties. There wasn't a single wrinkle on her face. Her blonde hair didn't have a visible speck of gray in it. A quick glance on her social media would tell you she spent just as much time in the gym as her professional football playing son. Marathon training now filled her days.

"I think so too," I admitted about the dress. "And, I know I said we didn't need to do all of this...but, thank you. All of you. For being here. It kind of made me forget how nervous I was for a bit."

"Nervous?" Ruth scoffed. "What on earth do you have to be nervous about? Jake adores you."

"I messed up six years ago. Pretty bad," I began, letting out a breath.

I'd never talked to my mom or abuela at length about Jake. Not like this. I think at this point, it was safe to say that everyone knew there was something more than friendship between us. I never spoke of it, though.

"When Jake kissed me, I panicked. Feeling something as strongly as I did for Jake at eighteen—or as I *do*—was terrifying. I had never felt that before. I haven't felt anything like it since. What I feel for your son scares me. I'm just not running from it anymore."

My mother's silence following my admission surprised me. Until I realized she was letting Ruth take this one because she knew how important it was for the two of us to bond. Out of the three women sitting together on the sofa, my mom knew both me and Jake—collectively and separately—the best. She was not his mom. She never tried to be, but she played such a vital role in his life. Then and now.

"Jacob has been sure of two things in his life: football and you." Ruth's lips curled into a smile. When her phone started to ring in her purse, she pulled it out, laughing once she saw the name on her screen. "Hi, Jake."

After retreating into the dressing room, I quickly changed out of the dress and back into the clothes I had borrowed from my mother earlier. When I emerged, Ruth was saying goodbye to my mom and abuela. "Jake's going to pick me up outside in ten minutes. He got me a meeting with a realtor and wants me to meet with him before I head back to Florida."

When Jake told me his mom had decided to move back to Fox Hollow, he had been so excited. My family served as his second family for a long time, but no one would ever be able to replace his mom.

I thanked Ruth for coming, which she completely brushed off. "No, thank *you* for letting me tag along."

As soon as Ruth walked out of the dressing room, my mom stood up and pulled me into her arms. I hugged her back, but there was no way to mask my concern as we put space between us after the embrace.

"What was that for?" I asked, looking over to Abuela for some sort of hint.

"I understand why you didn't tell me about Jake," my mom started. "But I wish you didn't have to go through that alone, mija. I knew you had a crush on Jake. Everyone knew. I didn't realize how much you loved him—how much you *love* him, though. If I had known..."

Abuela, who had been sitting there quietly, stood up and took my hand in hers. "No tengas miedo. Todo lo que necesitas es amor."

I didn't know it then, but her words would play back in my head repeatedly later that night.

"Don't be scared. Love is all you need."

ISA

BY THE TIME Ruth returned to my parents' house from the meeting with the realtor, I was sitting in the kitchen getting my face contoured by my mom's event aesthetician.

"If you go this big for a first date, I can't wait for the wedding day." Ruth chuckled as she took a seat in one of the empty chairs. "Not that I'm rushing it!"

At exactly six o'clock on the dot, my parents' doorbell rang.

Like a scene from a movie, my dad's face lit up in recognition. "Give me a second with him before you come in," he said. Then, he winked and grinned before making his exit out of the room.

"Daddy! Don't you dare!" I called out, causing a ripple effect of laughter from Mom, Abuela, and Ruth. Following behind him, I stopped short when I saw Jake.

The jacket of the slim-fitting navy suit he was wearing was open. It exposed the crisp white cotton dress shirt underneath. The top two buttons were undone, giving him a more relaxed look.

He laughed at something my father said but stopped abruptly when he saw me. His Adam's apple bobbed as he swallowed and shifted his body. "Wow, Isa. You look— no, you *are* beautiful."

"You're not so bad yourself." I grinned.

The moment was lost once Ruth came barreling into the room. "Wait! Before you go!" She held up her phone and shrugged. "I know this is lame, but I missed out on prom night. Both of them."

She pointed to the photographs of Jake and I that were taken on the nights of our junior and senior proms. I hadn't noticed until now that three photographs of me and Jake had made their return to the mantle.

When Wes and I started getting serious, he asked why there were photographs of me and Jake plastered all over my parents' house. Granted, there were only three—one from each prom and another from our high school graduation—but nevertheless, I told my mother it bothered him.

The next time we came over, the photos were gone.

"Ooooh!" Abuela exclaimed. "¡Afuera! ¡Junto a las rosas!"

"Okay, fiiiiine," Jake conceded, throwing his hands up in mock defeat. "But we have to make it kind of quick. Isa and I have to be there by seven."

To anyone else, this pre-date craziness would be, well, crazy. For me and Jake, it only seemed appropriate our family would be involved. Honestly, at this point, I was a little surprised my brother and Adam hadn't shown up too.

As we all headed to the backyard, my mom told the story of the rose trellises to Ruth, airiness in her voice as she recalled how my father decided instead of continually buying her favorite flowers for them to only die in a week or two, he would give her hundreds of red roses year after year. The white trellises lined the entire back fence of the yard—one of very few things my dad hired someone else to take care of.

My parents didn't have a housekeeper. My dad mowed the lawn every Saturday morning. He watered all the plants. My mom and abuela took care of the small vegetable garden. The roses had their own gardener, though. It was undeniably the most romantic thing I'd ever seen or heard of.

"Wow, Coach," Jake teased. "I didn't peg you for such a hopeless romantic."

"Wow, Jake," my dad mimicked Jake's tone before narrowing his eyes in Jake's direction, "I didn't peg you for a guy that wanted to lose his girlfriend's dad's approval before you even left for your first date."

Jake laughed as his hand slid across my back. "Fair enough."

His fingers curled, gripping ever so slightly at my waist. I rested my hand flatly on his chest. They were two very simple gestures we'd done in pictures together before. This time was different, though. It was possessive.

His hands were on me. He had a smile that stretched from ear to ear. His shoulders were back, relaxed. He was happy.

I knew as soon as we'd step out of the car that night, this little happy bubble we were in would pop. There was already speculation on the Internet about our relationship because of the parking lot kiss. I told Jake I didn't care what anyone said about me, about us, but the urge to see what everyone was saying had been stronger than my willpower.

I looked while I was getting my hair curled. Some of the things people said were enough to make me question whether or not I could handle this. Jake was a public figure. Part of being in a relationship with him would mean we'd be subject to public scrutiny.

I didn't care what anyone said about my looks; it was the comments made about my character. Words like *"gold-digger"* and *"using him"* stuck out like flashing neon lights.

I almost canceled on Jake. But before I did, I had asked the only person I *knew* would understand: my mama.

She started dating my dad right after *his* rookie season with the Bluecoats. While she didn't necessarily have to deal with it at the extreme that I would, even thirty years ago people felt the need to throw their opinions around carelessly.

"You have to ask yourself one thing, mija." she started. "Do you love him? If the respuesta es sí, it's worth it. Todo."

All it took was a single moment of motherly reassurance to put it all behind me.

Because he was worth it.

All of it.

JAKE

As Isa was saying her goodbyes, Coach pulled something out of his pocket and handed it to me. *Keys.*

"Is this?" I asked with wide eyes.

The 1929 Ford Model A in the driveway wasn't the exact car Abuela had driven across the border when she fled from Mexico, but a gift Coach had given her for one of her previous birthdays. It was the only car that went into the garage at all times. And, I was obsessed.

Coach nodded. "Abuela insisted. I checked the oil and topped off the gas this morning. You should be good to go." He continued with, "I know I don't have to give you the big dad speech that I'm supposed to. Just take care of my girl, okay?"

"You have my word, Coach," I assured him as Isa began walking over to us.

"Abuela said we were taking her car!" Isa beamed, and my confirmation jingled in my hands. She leaned up and gave her dad a quick peck on the cheek. Lowly, she chuckled and said, "Wish me luck, Daddy."

"Luck? What do you need luck for?" he asked. "You have Jake."

Opening the passenger side door, I stepped back and waited until Isa and her dress were all the way in the car before closing the door. I turned to wave to Coach one last time and laughed when I saw our moms and Isa's abuela had joined him on the front lawn to see us off.

Once we were both situated in the car, I turned to Isa and smirked. "Ready?"

"Ready as I'll ever be." Her smile in response was small, her voice quiet and timid. Nothing like the Isa I knew.

"What's wrong?" I shifted in the seat to face her. "And don't say 'nothing'...I know you better than that."

She chuckled. "I guess I'm just nervous. I've been in the football world my whole life, but not like this. I've always been someone's daughter. Tonight, I'm someone's girlfriend."

It never occurred to me that she would feel nervous about tonight. She had walked the red carpet at the ESPYs. Coach Coleman brought her as his plus one to multiple Hall of Fame induction ceremonies. I just assumed she would look at tonight like all those nights.

"It's just..." She broke eye contact with me and sighed. "I'm not a model. Or an actress. I'm just me."

"That's my favorite thing about you," I said as I took her hands in mine. "That you're you."

"Jake." She rolled her eyes and shook her head. "I'm being serious."

"So am I," I started. "You are my favorite person on this earth, Isabel. You're kind. You're tenacious. You're patient. You're talented. You're smart. You're beautiful, inside and out. I feel like the luckiest guy in the world because I get to walk in that room tonight with you on my arm."

Her eyes searched mine. She was looking for a lie to call me out on. Unfortunately for her—or maybe actually it was fortunately for her—there were no lies to be found.

In the entire time we'd known each other, I'd never been able to look her straight in the face and lie to her. In the beginning of our friendship, usually when it came to other girls or things I wasn't exactly *proud* of, I would break eye contact, laugh, or ramble my bullshit so fast in hopes she wouldn't see through it. But she did. Every damn time.

Eventually, I just stopped lying to her. Not only was it pointless, but I hated doing it. Keeping the truth from her always left me feeling sick to my stomach. Isa deserved the truth.

"You mean it," she said when she realized everything I just told her was true.

"Of course I mean it," I confirmed. "So, what do you say, Bug? You ready?"

This time, her smile was genuine as she nodded. "I'm ready."

ISA

The Fairgrounds had lived on Wickett Pond Drive for as long as I could remember.

The six-bedroom, loft-style house had direct access to Wickett Pond. When we were younger, Matt and I would take the pathway from their backyard and spend all day at the pond. No matter what he said, seven-year-old me was convinced they lived in a castle and were secretly royalty.

It wasn't just the cathedral ceilings, multiple fireplaces, French doors, and hardwood flooring; the Fairgrounds family had a live-in maid, a chef, a house manager, and a gardener. Matt went to a private, all-boys Catholic school. They threw the most elaborate parties. Matt's birthday parties were weekend-long celebrations. But even the circus-themed birthday that had clowns, magicians, and live animals under a red and white striped big top seemed small in comparison to the way the backyard was set up now.

As soon as we stepped over the threshold, a loud gasp greeted us.

"Oh, my heart!"

To just about everyone else tonight, the couple that stood greeting their guests as they arrived were Hugh and Pauline Fairgrounds: owners of the Boston Bluecoats. But to me, they were my godparents. Matt's mom and dad. My parents' best friends.

"Hi, Godparents!" I said, greeting the two of them.

"I was just over the moon when your mom called to tell us you were coming as Jake's date tonight." Pauline's red lips curled upward in a big, bright smile. "You look like a princess!"

"I feel like a princess," I admitted as Hugh pulled me in for a hug.

"Ready for the photo op?" he asked quietly, though the question was rhetorical. More like a warning of sorts. When he pulled back, he very loudly said, "Who would have thought. My godchild, the only daughter of Roger Coleman, here with my MVP."

Right on cue, the event photographer stepped forward. "How about a group shot?"

Immediately, I noticed the Canon EOS 5DS the photographer had in his hands and smiled. A few weeks ago, Hugh had called me and asked for camera recommendations. He wanted to make sure his staff had the best of the best for this event.

With Hugh on one side of me and Jake on the other, I flashed a smile for the camera. After the photo was taken, Jake and I began to make our way toward the large tent in the backyard.

There wasn't time to appreciate the large floral arrangements, the white dance floor with the Bluecoats logo painted on it, or the clear top of the tent before Jake and I were bombarded by his teammates.

JAKE

AFTER TAKING OUR SEATS, I exhaled. A small glass box with my name engraved into it sat on top of the blue tablecloth. The biggest ring I'd ever seen in my entire life was behind the glass. Sure, I'd seen Roger Coleman's Super Bowl rings, but they weren't anything like the one tucked behind the glass in front of me.

"Whoa," Isa whispered as she took the seat next to mine and looked over into the box. Squeezing my arm gently, her voice was still hushed when she continued. "I'm so damn proud of you."

Six syllables, making up six little words.

That was all it took.

Tears filled my eyes to the brim and threatened to fall freely.

Maybe it had to do with reaching a career high. The finale of my very first Super Bowl win was beginning. A celebration of victorious triumph that was enough to bring even the toughest of men to tears.

Or maybe it was having this very woman by my side this evening. Out of the trillions of people in the world, there wasn't anyone I'd rather have next to me than Isabel Coleman.

Turning to face her, I knew there was a chance this may not be reciprocated. It didn't matter, though. She needed to know. If the last six years showed me anything, it was that time stopped for no one, and everything could change in a single moment.

"I love you." The words fell from my lips effortlessly. We'd said it to each other hundreds of times during the duration of our friendship, but never like this. "Like, I *really* love you."

Her lips curled as she studied me for a moment. "I really love you too."

There wasn't time to soak up our moment before the table began to fill with players. Once everyone had settled in their seats, Hugh and Matthew Fairgrounds took turns welcoming everyone from the front of the tent.

"Congratulations, champions," Hugh began, grinning. "Now, put those rings on and let's fucking party! Here to kick off the night's celebration—my good pal, Snoop Dogg!"

The room erupted in cheers and laughter after Hugh's introduction, and gasps and phrases like "*oh my God*" were heard around the table as my teammates started to take their rings out of the glass boxes.

Out of the corner of my eye, I saw Isa hold her phone up. Turning, I faced her, and she nodded in response.

"Go on," she nudged. "Open it."

With that, I opened the box in front of me and took the silver ring into my hand. Meticulously, I inspected the ring. Diamonds. A Lombardi Trophy on one side, our team logo on the other. Sliding it onto my right ring finger, I raised my hand to my face and offered Isa a smile. Right on cue, she snapped a photo.

A snowball effect took place with players around the table, asking Isa to grab photos of us together. Fox and Lynx—who'd brought their mom and little brother as their plus ones—gathered around me.

"Make sure you text that to me!" Fox said before he extended his hand and offered to take a picture of me and Isa.

"I'll just send it to Jake." Isa smiled. "I don't have your number."

"Well, let's change that," Fox said, as he tapped on Isa's phone screen repeatedly. "Now you do!"

"Mattyyyyy!" Isa called out as Matt Fairgrounds joined our table. At the sight of our old friend, the nervous tension that had settled in her shoulders seemed to disappear a little.

"It's about time, you two. Took you long enough." Matt grinned, pointing between me and Isa. "Come on. There's no way you're sitting in your seats while Snoop fucking D-O-Double-G is on the stage. Come on. Let's go."

What should have been a ten-second walk took us closer to ten minutes. We were stopped along the way. Introductions were made. Isa blushed when players recognized her as Roger Coleman's daughter. There was a gushing pride in her voice as she thanked them for the praise given to her in reference to her father.

Once we made it to the stage area, we danced. We sang. We ate our weight in street tacos. While most of the people around us were drinking champagne, Isa and I drank glasses of Fairgrounds Cranberry Co.'s very own sparkling juice.

"What do you say, Bug?" I asked for the second time tonight. "Ready to sneak out of here?"

ISA

We must have hit every damn red light between the Fairgrounds' house and Jake's. The universe was certainly toying with us as we drove across town. Quiet anticipation radiated off both of us once Jake pulled into his driveway.

His hands shook as he fidgeted with the keys to unlock the door. Quickly, he disarmed the home security system as soon as we walked through the threshold. As I closed the front door, he stripped out of his suit jacket, tossing it on the couch a few feet away.

A low chuckle left his lips as he looked down at my feet. "I'm surprised your heels lasted on your feet for as long as they have."

"I can't wait to get out of them," I admitted, laughing myself.

"I can't wait to get you out of that dress." Jake slyly grinned. "I mean, it's pretty and all, but…"

"Well, what are you waiting for?" I countered, a silent dare in my eyes as they swept over him.

One smooth stride told me that was all the permission he needed before he closed the space between us. His hands, hungry and hurried, found their way to my hips. A firm grip, a tug toward him, and his mouth landed on mine.

My hands were in his hair, then. A tug of their own as we collided in a crash of years' worth of wanting. I fumbled with the halter tie behind my neck, unable to remove it fast enough as I kicked one heel off, then the other. At once, I shrunk several inches from his grasp. He laughed, backing up, undoing the top button of his shirt, followed by the one below it.

I eyed him with amusement, biting back a smile on my lips, swollen from our fervent kiss. "What are you doing?"

A smirk played on his lips as he nodded toward my discarded heels. "Two for two. We're still keeping score, right?"

My only response was one last tug, and the slip of my dress.

ISA

I COULD FEEL Jake's eyes on me as I slowly stirred from sleep. Though I couldn't say for certain *when* we crashed. I felt a little delirious, a little high, apparently tending to be that way after multiple orgasms.

I would never confirm this to the thousands of strangers that commented about this on the regular, speculating publicly on social media...but yes, Jake looked even better *without* the uniform on. And he, in all his naked glory, was only mine to see.

"Good morning," I murmured, batting away the memory of his talented mouth all over me.

Jake leaned over and left a kiss on top of my head, and I sighed with content. "Move in with me," he said.

It didn't sound like a question, but after last night, I was willing to bet I'd give him whatever he asked of me—within reason. Sleepy laughter rolled off my lips as I looked up at him.

Jake's brow immediately furrowed in confusion.

"Oh. You were serious." I swallowed. "Jake, I can't move in with you."

"Why not?" he questioned.

"Because, it's been days, Jake. *Days*," I said softly. "Don't get me wrong, I've loved every second we've spent together. It's just too soon."

"Too *soon*? It's been years." He let out an exasperated sigh as he flung the covers back.

"I know things have moved fast with us," I continued, sitting up on the bed. "But, Jake, this is crazy."

"So, now I'm crazy?" He laughed in disbelief.

"That's not what I said," I shot back defensively. Reaching down to the floor, I pulled the T-shirt I stole from him last night up and over my naked body. This wasn't shaping up to be a conversation to have without clothes on. "Don't twist my words around."

"You just said you don't want to move in with me because what, you need space, right? What else do you need space from, Isa?" he paused, but not quite long enough for me to respond. "Yeah, that's what I thought."

"Jake, come on," I said, reaching for him. "You are overreacting. We're both running on very little sleep. Just, come back to bed."

"I have to take my mom to the airport," he said flatly, as he pulled a T-shirt from his dresser. "I'll just...I'll talk to you later. Lock up when you leave."

When. Not *if*.

Without another word, he left.

———

MY MOM ASKED me six times during the forty-five-minute drive to the airport what was wrong. I lied, telling her I was hungover and didn't get much sleep last night. At least the latter was the truth.

Last night was perfect. From the start at the Colemans to the end of the evening, when Isa fell asleep in my arms. Everything finally felt as it should be.

Right up until I asked her to move in with me.

And she laughed. She fucking laughed.

Maybe it was my own stubborn pride that made her response feel like a slap in the face.

Or, maybe, it was that the sinking feeling I'd had all along was true—that this didn't mean to her what it did to me.

I didn't want to wait to start our lives. We'd spent six years apart. All that time we could have been together was gone. There was no getting it back. Why wouldn't we be doing everything in our power to make up for lost time?

After dropping my mom off at the airport, I drove around Boston aimlessly. When my gas light lit up, I pulled into the first gas station I saw.

After pumping my gas, I stopped in the little store for a Gatorade. But when I walked up to the check-out counter—Gatorade in hand—I froze at the sight of my father's face on one of the tabloids.

"Football's Golden Boy Jake Pierce Leaves Father Homeless" read the headline.

Leaving the drink on the counter, I left the store. As soon as I was in the safety of my truck, I cursed.

"Fucuuuuuuuuuk."

My stomach tightened, anger filling me. The horn blasted as my fist made impact with my steering wheel. Before anyone caught on that it was me and managed to secure *another* bullshit story of tabloid fodder, I started my truck and made my way back to the highway.

About halfway back to Fox Hollow, the music cut out and my

Bluetooth speaker alerted me that I had an incoming phone call from Isa.

Answering it, I sighed. "I need to call you back."

"Jake, we need to talk," she said.

"I need to call you back," I repeated.

Isa and I may have had our own things to work through, but I needed to clear my head first.

"Why are you being like this?" she asked. Her voice changed with her question. It was accusatory. Angry. "All over me because I said I wouldn't move in? You cannot be serious."

"Fine," I conceded. "You wanna talk? I'll be home in twenty minutes. Let's fucking talk."

JAKE

"Hey," Isa said, offering me a small smile as she raised the aluminum pan in her hands. "Mom sent over your favorite: enchiladas and rice."

My silence greeted her as she placed the pan on the counter. Instead of acknowledging her, I downed the glass of bourbon I poured when I heard her open the door. She had been at her parents' house. I knew, because her car was parked in their driveway when I drove by.

She was still wearing my T-shirt from this morning. Her hair was pulled up in a loose, messy bun and she was wearing big, black glasses. I'd never, in the entire duration of our friendship, seen her wear glasses. If this was yesterday, I would have commented on how cute she looked in them, but all I could picture when I looked at her now was her sitting at the kitchen table with her mom and abuela—*laughing* at me.

"Jake? What's going on?" She tried to close the space between us, but I stepped back. "Is it the glasses?" she joked. "I know. I'm getting used to them, too. I got the call they were ready when you were bringing your mom to the—"

I knew if I didn't do this, I'd change my mind. I wouldn't say what I needed to say. "Isa, stop."

"I know we got in a fight but, come on." She swallowed. "We just have to talk about it."

"I don't think so. I think we need to take a step back." I exhaled, looking away from her. "I think we need to take a break."

"People don't take breaks, Jake." My heart raced as her voice began to shake. "People break up. Don't do this. Please, don't do this."

Each word she said felt like another slash to my heart.

I loved her. With every fiber of my being. Which was why I couldn't—I *wouldn't* allow myself to go down the road to the inevitable. I was ready to start my life with her. I had been waiting years for this.

She didn't want the same thing I did.

She laughed when I asked her to move in with me. A sound that usually brought me incredible joy had suddenly felt like a slap in the face.

Now, when I didn't say anything back, Isa's body shifted. A thin line spread across her lips as she crossed her arms. In a split second, the worry in her face disappeared.

In classic Isa style, she was going to deflect her pain. Act like she was fine. And then, as soon as she was by herself, she would allow herself to feel.

I knew this because more often than not, as teenagers, I would watch her build the safety wall around her heart when she thought people were going to hurt her.

I'd never been the one to cause it, though.

"So, is that it?" she asked, as if being in this kitchen with me was the last thing she wanted to do in that moment. "Is that all you wanted me to come over for? To break up? Because if we're done, I'd like to go."

"I'm sorry."

Those two little words were all I could think to say.

And, I was.

I was sorry for pulling her into this. I was sorry for letting my heart get the best of me. I wished we could just go back to last night—to slow dancing with her in my arms. Selfishly, I wanted to pull her into my arms again.

If I had known the kiss I placed on her lips this morning would be the last, I would have savored it. I would have taken my time. Memorized the shape of her curves, the feel of her skin against mine.

Shaking her head profusely, she raised her hand to stop me from saying anything more. "No. You don't get to do that. You don't get to feel sorry. If this is what you want, you're going to own it."

I opened my mouth to tell her that I truly *was* sorry, closing it when I realized it wouldn't make a damn difference.

"Isa..."

Before I could say another word, she turned on her heels. I winced as she slammed the front door shut. The sound of her tires spinning out of the driveway made me want to chase after her.

Instead, I shot back the bourbon and poured another...and another...

ISA

IT HAD BEEN three days since Jake ended things between us in his kitchen.

Not wanting to deal with the interrogation from my family, I checked into a hotel Monday night. I cried until there were no more tears to cry, passing out from exhaustion sometime around three in the morning.

When check-out time came, as much as I wanted to stay another night, I knew if I did my family would start to worry. All it would take would be one of them driving by Jake's house and only seeing his truck in the driveway and a conversation with my brother for my mother to start a search party.

For the first time in my career, I rescheduled a private photo session.

Not just one, but two. I had two families booked for photographs yesterday...and I sent them emails saying I was sick. *Broken hearts counted, right?*

And then, I lied to my brother.

When he realized I was still home this morning—and not off

surprising Jake in Green Bay like I planned—he flew into my room.

"You're going to miss your flight!"

Tonight was just a pre-season game, but it would have been Jake's first game I'd gone to since high school. As soon as Jake and I were "official," I bought tickets to the game and booked a flight to Wisconsin. Much like having his mom show up to training camp, I wanted to surprise him. Javier and Adam were the only two people who even knew I was planning on going.

Instead, I was still in Fox Hollow, hiding in my gallery space.

The permits I had pulled for renovations were approved on Monday—the day after Jake broke my fucking heart—and by Tuesday morning, the contractors were in here tearing shit down. Luckily for me, the game didn't start until six o'clock. So, by the time I got here, all of the workers had already cleared out for the day.

I tried to keep myself busy. Sitting in the lone office chair left by the previous owners, I opened my laptop with the intent of getting some work done, but ended up ordering birthday presents for Finn instead. I called in sushi, and once my volcano rolls were gone, I decided that the newly opened space would be the perfect place to skate.

Afterward, when I reached down into my bag for my car keys, I saw that my phone was lit up. I pulled it out to find the news alert from the Bluecoats app that they had won the game. Before I could stop myself, I was opening the app, looking at the stats of the game. When I saw Jake made the first and last touchdowns of the game, my eyes filled with tears.

Opening Instagram next was my first mistake. My second mistake was going straight to Jake's profile. There wasn't anything new posted, so I tapped on the tagged photos. But what I wasn't expecting to find was my name being tagged in a photograph of Jake, Fox, and Lynx surrounded by half-naked models. Glasses full of champagne filled their hands. A rush of déjà-vu washed over me. This felt like college all over again. Only this time, there were comments like: *"Where's Isa?"* and *"That doesn't look like Isa!"*

Neither of us had publicly commented on our breakup.

Until now, I had been secretly holding on to the hope that it wasn't real.

And, if it was, that it was temporary.

Any moment now, Jake would realize he made a huge mistake and we'd be back together again.

I decided I was done crying for the night. I had every intention of going home, but as soon as I saw the wooden sign for "Spirits & Ales" in worn gold lettering, I turned into the almost full parking lot.

The Claddagh Lounge was the local watering hole. Black-and-white checkered tiling, old wood paneling on the wall, bright-red cushioned barstools and the almost too-loud rock music that blasted from the three PA-style speakers scattered throughout the pub was exactly what I need tonight.

None of my family members would ever step foot in here—and that's why I loved it so much. Salem and I had spent many Thursday nights here after we turned twenty-one. I was always her designated driver. Which meant I always got to pick the karaoke songs we did.

It didn't matter that I didn't have a drop of makeup on or that my hair was thrown up in a messy bun. My ripped jeans and Camp Crystal Lake Counselor graphic tee didn't so much as earn me a second glance as I walked through the door and straight to the bar.

Before my ass even hit the cushioned seat, I was greeted by Erin—the curvy redhead that owned the pub.

"I'll be right over, Isa!" she called from the beer draft.

"I don't like that color on you."

After taking a seat on the empty stool on the other corner end of the bar, Devon McDaniels placed his half-empty beer on the scratched mahogany bar top.

"Excuse me?" I asked.

I was not in the mood for Devon fucking McDaniels and his bullshit games tonight.

"Blue," he answered, not skipping a beat as a tall pint glass full of ginger ale was placed in front of me.

I was glad that Erin remembered I didn't drink.

For a split second, I had thought about asking for vodka.

Devon picked up his beer like he was going to take a sip. He held it in front of his mouth, but the glass never made it to his lips.

"Devon, I'm not in the mood," I warned. What little patience I had for him and this conversation was fading. Fast. "Either tell me what you're talking about or, please, just leave me alone."

"You're more of a yellow. Blue doesn't suit you."

I was done, then. Both with Devon and this conversation.

As I stood and reached into my pocket for the cash I had shoved in there before coming in, Devon also stood. "Isa, wait."

"Blue," he began, placing his beer on the cardboard bar coaster. "Sad, upset, down in the dumps. You are normally like sunshine. Happy. Glowing. Yellow."

Before I realized what I was saying, I blurted out, "Not that it's any of your goddamn business, but Jake and I broke up."

It was the first time I had said those words aloud. I hadn't even told my family or Salem yet. When Javier asked why I wasn't in Green Bay with Jake, I lied. I told him I woke up with the worst cramps and didn't think "Aunt Flow" would have fun in Green Bay. I didn't even have my period night now. It was the same excuse I gave my dad when he called to see if I was going over to his house to watch the game.

They were my family, but they were also guys—who would not only not question it, but were more than happy to be done with the conversation if It meant they didn't have to talk about "*feminine problems*" as my dad so delicately put it before hanging up the phone.

Saying it was over made it seem final. Saying it made it feel real. I had been living in a state of denial. I didn't want to accept that it was over. We had just found each other again. I wasn't ready to let go.

But what other choice did I have? Relationships took two people, and Jake didn't want this. Jake didn't want *me*.

Devon's eyes widened in surprise at my admission. "I'm sorry. That sucks."

"Are you, though?" I laughed, calling bullshit on his apology. "Are you *really* sorry?"

"Absolutely." He nodded. "I don't like seeing you sad. Do you want to talk about it?"

I did, but not with Devon. It was just past nine. There was a good chance Salem was still awake. Once I was in my car, I would text her. If she didn't answer by the time I left Fox Hollow, I would go home, take a hot bath, eat an entire pint of ice cream, and watch *Breakfast at Tiffany's*.

"Not really." I shrugged and pointed to the door. "I'm gonna go."

In the short time I'd been there, the rock music had transitioned to karaoke night. A group of newly turned twenty-one-year-olds took over the small dance floor. While weaving my way in and out of them toward the exit, I was halted to a stop when someone tugged on my arm.

I turned around with the intention of telling whomever it was that I was leaving, I rolled my eyes when I saw Devon. Before I got a chance to say anything, he gripped my waist and pulled me to him. His lips crashed down on mine. Without even thinking, I sent my fist right into his stomach.

I needed to get the fuck out of there. But a tight grip on my arm stopped me from moving. While still keeping a tight hold on my arm, Devon stood in front of me.

"Devon." I gulped. "Let me go."

"Admit it," he whispered. His gray eyes had gone dark. The words sounded like a threat as he continued, "You wanted it. That's why you told me about the breakup. You wanted—"

Cutting him off, I shook my head. "No. That is not—"

"You and I have been dancing around this for years, Isa." He leaned in closer. The smell of the beer on his breath made my stomach turn. His grip tightened as he continued. "I'm tired of waiting."

Panic filled me. I knew I should kick, scream...anything to cause a scene. Yet, I stood there, frozen in place.

"Devon, please," I begged. "You're hurting me."

Relief flooded through me when I heard Erin's voice behind us. "Let her go, Devon."

As soon as his arm fell, I muttered a thank you and ran out of the pub as fast as my legs would carry me. Once I was safely in the comfort of my locked car, the tears I didn't realize I had been holding back began to fall. Warm, salty puddles of anger rushed down my cheeks as the steering wheel took a small beating from my fists.

Without even thinking, I called the first person who came to mind.

The only person I knew could make me feel safe.

It wasn't until the second ring on the other end of the line, that I remembered calling Jake wasn't an option anymore. I was just about to pull the phone away from the side of my face and hang up when I heard his voice come through the speaker.

"Hey, Bug."

That was all it took.

A sob escaped my lips as I tried to find the words. Any words.

"Oh, baby." He sighed. "Please don't cry. I fucked up. I was going to wait till I got back. I wanted to say this to your face. I'm sorry. I'm so sorry."

He was saying everything I wanted to hear. Everything I needed to hear. But in that moment, it didn't matter. I stifled another sob long enough to tell him what happened in the pub.

"I felt like I was paralyzed, Jake. I couldn't move. I couldn't scream. What if Erin hadn't stepped in?" I shuddered.

Until tonight, I thought Devon was an asshole, but I didn't know he was capable of doing what he had done. God only knew what else could have happened.

There was a pause. "I'll be home—"

Cutting him off, I sighed. "I know. I shouldn't have even called you. I just...I just needed to hear you tell me that I'd be okay. I don't even know how I'm supposed to drive home right now."

"First of all," he started, "you can always call me. Always. No matter what's going on with us. Are you still in Fox Hollow?"

When I said that I was, he asked if I thought I could drive the five miles to his house.

"I just booked a flight back home on the red-eye," he said. "I'll be there in four hours."

"You're coming home tonight?"

"My girl needs me." He said it as if it was the most simple answer in the world. "I gotta pack up my clothes and head to the airport, but I'll see you in a bit, okay? And, Isa?"

"Yeah?"

"I love you."

JAKE

If I didn't know that it would come back to bite me in the ass, my fist would have already been in the hotel wall.

I threw my clothes in the suitcase, not giving a single shit about the condition they went in.

That bastard. That lucky bastard. He should be thanking his guardian angel that I am hundreds of miles away right now.

The thought of him kissing Isa made me angry, but I could have let that shit go. I couldn't blame the guy for having for having feelings for her. I knew better than anyone how it felt to love Isabel Coleman. However, the second she pushed him away, that should have been the end of it.

He sure as fuck shouldn't have laid a hand on her. The thought of her standing there frozen in fear as he held her in place had me seeing red. I had four hours to get this anger in check. If I didn't, I was not going home to Isa. I'd be on the hunt for Devon McDaniels. I also had four hours to figure out how the hell I was going to make the last few days up to Isa.

After I ended things with Isa, the only time my heart had any reprieve was when I was suited up, on my turf. Running plays allowed me to forget about my broken heart for just a few hours. I channeled every ounce of desperation I felt into the game earlier today.

Fox and Lynx were the only ones that knew what happened. They tried to cheer me up last night when we got to Green Bay, but it didn't take either of them long to realize champagne and the company of a few of their model friends was not what I needed. We stayed just long enough to take some pictures.

We ended up buying a foam football at the Target down the street from the hotel and spent the rest of the night tossing it back and forth in the almost-empty parking lot. Once again, the two of them helped me come up with a plan to fix things with Isa. A plan that would have taken place when I got home. *Tomorrow.*

There was no way I was waiting until tomorrow to see her, though. Not after hearing the way her voice shook. Not after feeling the gut-wrenching agony of not being able to pull her into my arms and comfort her.

After putting the last of my things into my suitcase, I grabbed my phone then stopped by Fox's room next to mine, before heading down to hand my room card into the front desk.

On the way to the airport, I sent a few texts to Coach Robertson and members of the team so someone knew I went home. We always traveled to the away games as a team, but there were always a few players that elected to go right home after games. I'd never considered it before tonight. Something told me I'd be taking the red-eye back to Boston a lot going forward.

ISA

I wasn't quite sure when I fell asleep.

After I disarmed the home security system at Jake's, I rearmed it. As I made my way to Jake's room, I stripped out of my shirt, bra, and jeans. I went right to his T-shirt drawer, grabbing the first one on top, and pulled it over my head.

I lay down on the right side of the bed—Jake's side of the bed —and as soon as I rested my head on his pillow, I knew I could let out the breath I'd been holding since Devon grabbed me.

I was safe here.

"It's just me! It's just me!" Jake called out as the wailing screech of the alarm filled the house. Within seconds, the alarm stopped and the sound of Jake's phone ringing in his pocket replaced the noise.

"Hi," he answered. A pause, then he chuckled, and a grin spread across his face as he assured the alarm company everything was fine. "My girlfriend just forgot to tell me she set it."

My girlfriend.

Maybe it was the overwhelming emotions from earlier today. Maybe it was my exhaustion. But, my eyes welled with tears at those two little words.

"I'm sorry," I began to apologize as Jake stepped forward and wiped the tears from my cheeks.

"It's okay." He smiled. "They just wanted to make sure no one was breaking in."

"Can you say it again?" I asked.

I knew there was so much that needed to be talked about, but we could do that in the morning. Right now, I just wanted to fall into his arms. Before I could allow myself to relax, I had to know what I was waking up to in the morning.

"It's okay?" he repeated. "Let's get you back to bed."

"No." I shook my head and stopped him. "You called me your girlfriend."

His lips tilted in a small smile of understanding. "I did. I know we need to talk about what happened and I know it's not going to be easy, but if the last few days have taught me anything, it's that I would rather fight with you than spend the rest of my life without you. I can't do it. I won't do it."

Sighing contently, I fell into his chest. We stood in silence for a few minutes, his arms wrapped tightly around me. The security his very presence gave me was exactly what I needed to feel.

"Come on, *girlfriend*." He chuckled. "Let's go to bed."

Once we were settled, my head resting on his chest, Jake began to stroke my hair.

"Isa?" he asked quietly, as his fingers ran through my hair.

"*Yessss?*" I mimicked.

"I love you."

"I love you too."

EPILOGUE

Isa

One Year Later...

IT HAD BEEN six months since I moved into Jake's house—*our* house—and I still found myself wanting to pinch myself in the mornings to make sure this was real.

"You ready, Bug?" Jake called out as I tied the laces of the waterproof 'bog boots' he'd given me as a gift for our first Valentine's Day together. He even had a matching pair for himself. It was so cheesy. It was so *us*.

"I'll be right out," I yelled back, pulling my ponytail through the distressed Boston Bluecoats hat I decided to wear.

Before Jake and I were a couple, sports apparel had always been limited to jerseys on game day. But...more and more I found myself adding Bluecoats items to my wardrobe.

Since I wouldn't need money or my phone where we were going, I left everything right on my nightstand. I found myself walking slowly down the hallway, admiring the photographs we'd hung together just last night.

Some of my favorite moments of our first year were captured within the photos—Jake's second Super Bowl win, a family shot of us at Javier and Adam's wedding, horseback riding together in Montana, and most recently, our trip to Disney World with Finn and Salem. A birthday present for Finn from his favorite *uncle* Jake.

It hadn't always been easy.

During the off-season, Jake took matters with his birth father into his own hands. There was an ugly court battle with the tabloid that printed the story—the one that had pushed him over the edge when he ended things between us. Jake's publicist set him up with interviews on shows, from Good Morning America to Sports Center, to allow him to tell the truth—*again*. And then, when all was said and done, Jake finally started the therapy he needed to work through the *years* of emotional turmoil bestowed upon him by the (lack of) grace from his father.

Jack and I, as a couple, were still learning new things about each other.

It only took me a few weeks to realize not only did Jake still *not* like cooking—which was why he always hired someone to prepare his food before I moved in—he also didn't like doing the dishes. And, had no problem letting them stack up in the sink.

To be fair though, Jake wasn't exactly impressed when he came to discover that laundry was the very bane of my existence and I waited to do it until I had no other choice.

The one thing we agreed on was that Tuesday nights were date nights. It was the one night during football season he would never have a game. Plus, chances of travel were pretty slim that day, and unlike Friday nights, we weren't obligated to attend family dinners at my parents' house.

This Tuesday was different, though. Tomorrow night, after a year of construction, renovation, and securing all of the artwork, I would *finally* open Coleman Collective. So, tonight, instead of finding a new restaurant to try or a beach to explore while summer still graced us with its presence, Jake and I were heading to the bog.

"Nice boots." He grinned when I joined him in the kitchen.

Swiping my keys from the counter next to him, I shook my head when his hand swatted my behind.

"Nice butt," he teased.

I rolled my eyes but couldn't help returning the smile. "Are you ready?"

"You could say that," he said, chuckling as he made his way to the door.

His response didn't make sense but before I got the chance to ask him what he meant by it he added, "You don't need your keys, babe. I'll drive. I *want* to drive."

"Are you okay?" I asked. "You're acting weird."

"Yeah," he said, waving me off. "It's just been a while since we've been to the bog. I'm excited."

I could understand that. It had been a while. We'd been so busy building our life together that we hadn't gotten the chance to slow down and visit the place that was so special to both of us.

Once I was settled in the passenger seat of Jake's truck, I noticed *the* picnic basket from the first dinner I had over at the house, sitting on the seat behind the driver.

"What's in the basket?" I asked, as Jake started the truck.

"Don't open it!" he practically shouted as he turned placing his hand on the headrest of my seat.

"I never said I was going to." I eyed him suspiciously as he backed out of the driveway. "What's going on with you? And don't say *nothing* because I know when you're lying, Jacob James."

He let out a small laugh and shrugged. "Okay, you caught me. I wanted to pack a special lunch—a celebration of sorts—to commemorate your incredible achievement of opening your own gallery. I'm just really proud of you and I know we won't have time to make a big deal out of it tomorrow."

Adoration for the man next to me filled me to the brim. "You're kind of perfect, you know that?"

Following up my question with a question of his own, Jake asked, "You know what song I haven't heard in a while? 'I Miss You.'"

"The blink-182 song?" I questioned, though I was sure there couldn't possibly be another song he was referencing.

"That's the one," he said as he reached for and then handed me his phone from the center console. "Wanna put it on for the few minutes we have left till we get to the bog?"

I obliged his request. Though, I was baffled by the randomness of it. It was easily put to the back of my mind as Jake slid his hand in mine. We never said it or made it "official" by any means, but ever since the night we both admitted that the song had reminded us of the other during those years we didn't talk, it had become *our* song. At least to me.

Somehow, as if he had timed it perfectly, the song ended just as we pulled into the parking lot of The Bog House.

"Should we go in and say hi?" I suggested, noticing Hugh Fairgrounds' SUV parked in the far end of the parking lot.

"How about after?" Jake said as he pulled into a parking spot, once again answering my question with a question. "I just don't want the food to spoil in the heat."

"After works for me," I said as I unbuckled and hopped down onto the concrete below.

The moment I saw the woods peeking out from behind the bog house, butterflies began to flutter in my stomach. Now I understood what Jake meant when he said he was just excited to be going back here. It just took me being here to realize it.

With the picnic basket in one hand, Jake offered me his other. We walked hand in hand until we got to the opening of the bog trail. With unexplainable reluctance, I let go of his hand and led the way down the path that'd take us to the fallen tree we'd claimed as our own.

Once we were both sitting, Jake placed the basket down on the ground between us. "Go ahead, I know it's killing you not to know what's inside of there."

Since there was no point in denying it, I opened the lid of the basket. Confusion settled in immediately when I realized there was no food in the basket. "There's nothing in there? Jake, what's going on?"

A small grin began to form on his lips when he asked, "Are you sure? Maybe reach all the way in the back."

I did as he suggested, and sure enough, my hands felt something small in the very back corner of the basket—a small black ring box.

My throat tightened at the very idea of what could be happening right now. I sure as fuck didn't want to be wrong in assuming, though. "Jake, what is this?"

"Oh, thaaaaat," he said as he gently took it out of my hand. "That's the ring I'm going to ask you to marry me with."

When he opened the box, I gasped. As he took the round cut ruby ring from the box, my heart raced. I was suddenly very thankful that he decided to do this while I was sitting down.

"Bug," he started, taking my left hand in his. "You are my very best friend. You are my family. My whole heart. I love you more than anything—even football—and I would love nothing more than to spend the rest of my life proving that to you. Isabel Coleman, will you marry me?"

"I love you more than football" I repeated back to him. "And nothing would make me happier than being your wife."

As he slid the ring on my finger, tears of joy fell freely down my cheeks. When the ring was securely placed onto my finger, I pulled his face to mine with my free hand. Just as our lips touched, the sound of crunching earth behind us grabbed my attention.

"Did you really think I was going to be able to pull this off without them?" Jake laughed at the sight of my parents, Ruth, my brother, Adam, and Abuela making their way down the trail. "I tried to tell them we would just come to the house afterward. There was no need for Abuela to come down here, but she wasn't hearing any of that."

"I wouldn't have it any other way," I told him, after I stole a quick kiss before everyone got to us. "By the way, you win. All of it. There's no more keeping score. I could never top this."

Isa, in love.

Jake, forever.

ACKNOWLEDGMENTS

As always, the first person I have to thank is my husband, Jeffrey. Thank you for all of my lattes and for holding my hand...and picking up the slack...as I wrote, mommed, and facilitated remote learning during a pandemic. Team Lagasse for the win, but let's be real...YOU THE MVP. I love you endlessly, Cracker Jack!

The Minis: Dillon, Kallie, and Hunter. I LOVE YOU THE MOST.

My family, especially my siblings. Thank you for always standing in my corner.

The team at Savage Hart Book Services, per usual, you ladies are a dream to work with. Thank you, Christina, Kat, Amanda, and Jen, for being on top of your game. Let's keep doing this together, okay?

Victoria Ellis. My work wife! Thank you for letting me bounce ideas off you, helping me dig myself out of plot holes, and being there to "squeee" over the exciting moments...and, you know, all that jazz.

Travis Soucy. The best of all best friends. Thank you for not giving me (too much) crap when it takes me five to ten business days to answer your texts, and for still being the same person since we were twelve. I don't know what I would do without you!

Chelsea Davis and Abbi Sullivan. If I were cool enough to have a squad, you two would be it. I don't know how I got so lucky to have not just one, but *two* partners in crime—and, by "crime" I obviously mean eating tacos and drinking margaritas during our wild moms' nights out—but I am thankful for it every day.

Daniele Derenzi, AKA the only human that has read every single version of this book. Thank you for your faith in Jake and Isa. Thank you for your faith in me.

Autumn Wrought. Thank you for always being there to lend a hand, an ear, or to moderate Dee's Bees when I need to step away from social media to write. You're such a bright light in my life.

Cristina Bon. There is no way I could have written this one without you. Thank you so much for reading *Keeping Score* early and for making sure I did right by Isa and her family.

My alpha and beta team: Vicci Kaighan, Haley Dauel, Tricia Ciak, Amanda Modschiedler, and Julie Moss. Thank you so much for giving me your time and your feedback! I am so grateful to have people I can count on to tell me when I need to both step up my game AND to cheer me on when I've succeeded. I appreciate all of you!

Dee's Bees. My favorite little corner of the book world. Thank you for always being there with Taron Egerton GIFs, music on Fridays, and to hype me and my books up.

Thank you to all of the bookstagrammers, bloggers, and readers who read ARCs, made graphics/teasers, and shared their love for Jake and Isa. You make my whole world go round.

Though they'll never see this, the fellas of blink-182. Thank you for being the first band that made me *really* fall in love with music. There is no better feeling than watching your favorite band live—

something I wrote about in *Keeping Score*. But, I personally learned that for the first time seeing blink as a teenager at Warped Tour. Thank you for music, and the memories.

And *you*. You took a chance on Jake and Isa. You took a chance on me. You're amazing.

ABOUT THE AUTHOR

Dee Lagasse is a mom of three from New England. When she's not writing, Dee can be found stalking The Royal Family, reading Marvel comics, or harassing her husband to reach something on the top shelf.

www.deelagasse.com

Email: dee@deelagasse.com

OTHER BOOKS BY DEE LAGASSE

Capparelli & Co

Without Warning

As Fate Would Have It

West Brothers

Meet Me Halfway

According to Plan

Kismet: A Royal Romance

Kismet Ever After : A Royal Short Story

Made in the USA
Monee, IL
07 February 2024

53122531R00120